First Published 2025

ISBN 13: 978-1-946738-94-3

Steel and SWAGGER

MariaLisa deMora

DEDICATION

"There's no crime in giving yourself over to pleasure."
~ Dr. Frank-N-Furter
The Rocky Horror Picture Show

For Andy, You were smart, funny, gritty, full of life, and deserved better than that little town ever gave you.

Contents

Chapter One...1

Chapter Two 6

Chapter Three 13

Chapter Four...32

Chapter Five...38

Chapter Six...42

Chapter Seven...48

Chapter Eight 50

Chapter Nine...52

Chapter Ten 62

Chapter Eleven...70

Chapter Twelve 74

Chapter Thirteen...77

Chapter Fourteen...80

Chapter Fifteen 87

Chapter Sixteen...93

Chapter Seventeen 102

Chapter Eighteen 174

Chapter Nineteen 195

Chapter Twenty 202

Chapter Twenty-One 211

Chapter Twenty-Two 251

Chapter Twenty-Three...260

ACKNOWLEDGMENTS

Thank you to Hot Tree Editing for continuing to work with me. Thank you to the readers who've stood next to me as I make my way back to the healed world. Thank you to my dear friends who've supported me through the struggles of the past couple of years.

Without each of you, I wouldn't have been confident enough to try writing again. It's certainly been a trip!

Woofully yours,
~ML

Steel and Swagger

Steel and Swagger follows the intense and passionate journey of Cherry, government name Tom Palant, a hardened Marine veteran turned enforcer for the Incoherent Motorcycle Club (IMC), and Denis Chapin, a sharp-witted lawyer with a heart of gold. Set against the bayou backdrop of Baton Rouge, the story delves into the complexities of identity, loyalty, and love.

Cherry, known for his iron will and fierce loyalty to the IMC, has buried his true self behind a wall of muscle and menace. But when he steps into Baton Rouge's hottest queer club, he meets Denis, a charismatic lawyer who sees through Cherry's tough exterior. As their worlds collide, Cherry and Denis navigate the treacherous waters of their burgeoning relationship, facing external threats from rival motorcycle clubs and internal struggles with their own identities.

As the IMC faces escalating tensions with a rival club, Cherry must balance his duty to his club with his desire for a life with Denis. The stakes are high, and the consequences of their choices could be deadly. Will Cherry and Denis find a way to reconcile their worlds, or will the pressures of their respective lives tear them apart?

Chapter One

Cherry

He stood there, boots planted firm on the worn hardwood of his Baton Rouge bedroom, staring down his reflection in the full-length mirror like it was an adversary he could intimidate into submission. One last long look, dragging his gaze over every detail. He had his sleeves rolled just so, creased crisp over thick forearms, the riot of ink spilling across his skin in a story told in color and shadow.

Cherry was Tom Palant to the government, but that name hadn't fit him comfortably in years, not since leaving the Corps. He tilted his head, catching sight of the wild thump of his pulse jumping under the taut skin of his throat. Too fast, too loud, like a war drum in his ears. He sucked in a breath, slow and deliberate, boxing it in his chest. Four in, hold, four out. Just like they'd drilled into him at Parris

Island, boxing it in his chest until the roar dulled to a growl.

There's still time to back out.

The thought slithered through his skull, slick and sly, and he blew out a rough sigh, fogging the mirror's edge. He didn't like it, even thinking it felt like quitting, but it was true enough. Not a single soul would blink if he didn't show tonight. All the way over to downtown Baton Rouge, in that club, with *that* crowd? Not a soul in his orbit had more than a passing clue he'd even consider it.

He'd buried that part of himself deep long ago, locked it behind a wall of muscle and menace, because the world he had served in, and now rode through, mostly didn't take kindly to shades of gray. They were leather and steel and lived by the Incoherent MC code that didn't bend.

But the club, and his crew inside those ranks, the tight circle he'd carved out? Busk, Rook, Diesel, hell any of those men, all of his brothers, were different. Open minds, with exposure to relationships that didn't follow the rules of the norm. So, they'd be at least open enough if he could screw up the courage. There had been too many decades of hiding, and now he'd finally found the ones who wouldn't flinch. At least, not too hard. If he ever let the truth slip.

Walking past, he gave his vest a reverent pat, fingers lingering on the patches before leaving it hanging off the back of the chair. These colors were his lifeblood, stitched into his soul as sure as the ink on his skin. Too precious to risk tonight, though, no way he'd drag the IMC's story into a place where it might get twisted up in questions he wasn't ready to answer.

The patch for his road name "Cherry" sat proud under the bold "Enforcer" nameplate, a warning in black and white that said "don't fuck with me." Inside the club or out, he was the steady hand, the iron fist using words first, posture second, and when that failed, knuckles did the talking. Below that patch was "Semper Fi 1775" which was a nod to the Corps, to the creed etched into his bones. The belief once a Marine, always a Marine.

The back told the rest of the tale in fractured but sharp pieces: "Incoherent MC" arcing across the top, the blue-winged eagle glaring fierce in the center, and "Baton Rouge" anchoring it all below. The IMC owned the Gulf coast, a sprawling empire from Florida's Big Bend to beyond the Texas line, every mile between claimed and held, by violence if needed. The Mother chapter was housed over in Hammond, just a spit from New Orleans, where the big dogs ran the show. Cherry didn't need to be there to feel the weight of it. The club was in his veins, every patch a scar he wore proudly.

Mid-prep, Cherry paused, a memory flickering.

Parris Island, his bunkmate Tommy's laugh cut through the humid dark, shirtless and careless, leaving Cherry's gut twisting with a want he'd choked down faster than a thought.

"Never again," he'd sworn, but here he was, breaking that vow.

He rolled his shoulders, forcing the tension down and away, glaring into the mirror as if he could bully himself into courage. The eyes staring back were hard, storm-gray, and pissed; his lips twisted into a silent snarl. "If not now, then when? Then when?" he rasped out, voice low and raw, the sound swallowed by the empty room. His hand dipped to the pockets of his skintight jeans, verifying the presence of keys, wallet, and yeah, a condom and lube, because hope was a stubborn bastard. "Been waiting my whole damn life for this." One last glare, a dare to the man in the glass. "Time to fucking own it."

Twenty minutes later, he stepped out of the rideshare, boots hitting pavement with a thud that echoed in his chest. The line snaked ahead, men jostling and laughing, all waiting for the bouncer's nodded invitation into the pulsing heart of Baton Rouge's hottest queer club. Cherry squared his shoulders and fell in, the night air sharp against his skin, carrying the faint tang of sweat and promise.

Chapter Two

Denis

The bassline thumped through the walls, chasing a couple into the bathroom as Denis Chapin gave himself a quick once-over in the smudged mirror, and approved of what he saw. His hair was still sharp, the shirt crisp enough. He grinned at the muffled grunts and moans already leaking from the big stall. *Good for them.* He shoved his tie into his jacket pocket, slipping back into the club.

The environment of the bar hit like a fist, a glorious roar of heat and sound. Too damn long since he'd busted out and shed the skin of the day. He was a public defender turned private gig, a grind of hard cases and rare wins, but today? That had been a fucking win. Court ended with his client walking free, and Denis watched the stress bleed out of the man's muscles with every stride. And the cherry on top was that same client's pregnant fiancée, waiting with open arms at the bottom of the courthouse steps.

That was glorious. Didn't hurt that there was a broad gaggle of press present.

Tomorrow's news coverage would bring more requests for representation, and having that knowledge felt fucking good.

Denis had cut his teeth as a public defender, spending a full decade noble and broke. He'd finally had a gut full of the kind of thankless defending that most days, left him feeling just a little bit greasy. Pulling the trigger on the change had been scary, but private work paid the rent now. Paid it and then some, so he could still throw in a bit of pro bono on the side when guilt gnawed. Today's win was sweet, and he'd needed that...and this. Blowing off work tensions in a way that felt very, very good, but had zero ties.

Been there, done that. Won't chase a man again.

He cut through the crowd to the bar, catching the bartender's eye with a flick of his chin. Pointed at a mid-shelf vodka, nothing fancy, just honest, and held up two fingers. A nod came back, and Denis turned, planting his elbows on the rail, back to the bar. The dance floor sprawled out before him, a sea of bodies gleaming under the lights. Some shirts already shed, those chiseled chests slick with sweat, grinding solo or tangled up in twos and threes. A twink near the center had two bears boxing him in, head lolling back on one's shoulder while the other yanked his hips forwards, guiding him into a shameless hump against a thick thigh. Denis smirked. *Live your truth, kid.*

"Ten," the bartender called, and Denis shifted to see a glass of iced vodka hit the bar. It was way more than two fingers, the pour was generous as hell. He fished his card from his pocket, flashing a grin that got him a flirty wink in return. The guy spun to the register, card in hand, and a minute later slapped a receipt down with a pen. Denis scribbled a fat tip. *Why not?* He flipped the paper, jotting his number on the back with a matching wink. An easy try, even if it didn't result in any fun.

"Oh, honey, you're the best," the bartender purred, brushing fingers over Denis' knuckles as he swept past to the next thirsty soul.

Still grinning, Denis turned back to the floor, and that's when he saw him. It was a new guy, skirting around the edge of the crowd, slow-dancing to a beat that wasn't playing with hands up, swaying like he was lost in some private song. Tattoos spilled down his arms, vivid against the rolled sleeves of a half-buttoned shirt, just enough chest hair peeking out to tease. He was fit and lean, and his posture hinted at something more than the normal club rat. Denis damn near bit his fist when the guy turned, tight jeans hugging an ass worth poetry. Another sway, a turn, and holy hell, the front was a revelation. The man's cock thick and unmistakable, outlined like a promise along his thigh. *God almighty.*

He slammed the vodka back, throat burning, and abandoned the glass with a clink. Weaving through the crowd, he threw a raised brow and headshake at another guy angling the same way.

Nope. Back off, pal.

He got a knowing grin as the dude peeled off. Denis slid in close, heat pouring off Tattoo like a furnace, and ghosted his hands along the man's frame, settling at the dip of his waist. No flinch, no jump. There was just a steady roll of hips that said he'd seen Denis already. *Permission enough.* Denis pressed in, chest to back, matching the rhythm, his own cock thickening as it grazed that poetry-worthy ass. Tattoo added a beat, one hand curling back to grip Denis' neck, and the room tilted.

The music slowed, piano notes curling through the air, and Tattoo flowed with it, spine arching against Denis' front. Too hot, too close, and yet not close enough. Denis slid a hand down, palm flattening over a ridged six-pack, fingers slotting into the grooves like they were made for it. Tattoo's hand twined with his, tightening, and a rough chuckle rumbled out, deep enough to vibrate through Denis' bones. Pants straining, Denis ducked his head, nipping the edge of Tattoo's ear, earning another laugh that hit like a shot of lust straight to his core.

"I like that, Suit Guy." Tattoo twisted, pressing into the touch, the move guiding Denis' lips to the sharp angle of his cheek. "What else you got?"

"Depends on what you're chasing, Tattoo. Me, I'm after some stress relief, need to blow off steam." Denis kissed a path from cheek to temple, then pulled back, locking eyes. "You?"

"Same deal." Tension flickered around Tattoo's eyes, a flash of something raw and jagged. He sucked in a breath, hard and fast, then used the grip on Denis' neck to spin, staying caged in his arms. His voice was low and reluctant when he spoke again, "Kinda out of my depth here, Suit Guy."

Denis eased back an inch, feeling Tattoo's hold tighten for a split second before loosening. "If you're just dipping a toe in, there's easier ways to test the waters."

Tattoo shook his head slow, gaze steady on Denis. "Not testing. Just...green. Semi-green. Don't have much experience like this. Out in public."

Denis arched into him, hips rocking, and grinned at the matching hardness he found. "Well, hell then." He leaned close, stubble scraping as he traced Tattoo's jaw, chasing those full lips. Tattoo groaned, turning into it, and Denis teased with a darting flick of tongue, swiping corner to corner, coaxing. The music shifted, rowdy and fast, and they moved with it, synced tight. Their lips brushing, hands roaming, hips locked. Denis pulled back to watch him move, and Tattoo's mouth parted, tongues grazing for one electric second. Eyes shut, face taut with want, Tattoo leaned close, and Denis crashed into him, claiming that open mouth with a hunger that drowned out the club. Tongues tangled, wet and fierce, and the world shrank to the ragged sounds spilling between them, the groans, the gasps, everything.

Chapter Three

Cherry

This is everything. The words looped in Cherry's head, a mantra sinking deep as the kiss burned hotter. From a tentative brush to a wildfire, it scorched through him, setting every nerve ablaze. *Everything.* Bodies jostled them, and he shuffled closer, plastering their chests together, cursing the layers of fabric keeping skin from skin.

Suit Guy broke away, eyes sparking as he grinned wide. "How about somewhere more comfortable? A lot more private." Those lush, sinful lips beckoned, but he dodged Cherry's dive for more. "Easy, gorgeous. Let's walk." Fingers laced, he tugged Cherry towards and through the exit, the club's chaos fading behind them.

Outside, the night air hit like a slap, cool against the sweat beading his face. Suit Guy steered them down the sidewalk, leaning close, cheek brushing Cherry's temple. The height difference registered then, funny how he'd missed it in the haze. "I'm just down here," Suit Guy murmured, voice a low hum. "Got lube, condoms, couple of cold beers in the fridge." He slowed, steps faltering. "If that's not your speed, no sweat. We can crack a beer and just talk shit, blow off steam that way."

"Beer's a start," Cherry said, pouring steel into his tone. "We'll feel it out from there. I'm in." He tipped his head up, catching that easy smile, and surged onto his toes for a kiss. Suit Guy met him halfway, deep and sure, and their steps stuttered to a stop. Cherry's fingers skimmed the man's jaw, trailing down his neck, every scorching touch stoking the ache coiling tight in his gut.

"Let's keep the PDA PG," Suit Guy teased, stepping back, one hand slipping free. He swept an arm towards the steps behind him. "This is me."

***

The stairs were solid under Cherry's boots, each step a deliberate thud that matched the hammer of his pulse. Suit Guy, who was still nameless, still almost entirely a mystery, led the way, his broad back filling his jacket, pulling tight across shoulders that promised strength. Cherry's eyes snagged on the flex of muscle, the way the fabric draped along his frame, and he swallowed hard, shoving his hands into his pockets to keep from reaching out. It was too soon, and his nerves were too raw. Plus, this wasn't his turf, and he wasn't about to stumble like some green prospect on his first ride.

At the top, Suit Guy fished keys from his jeans, the jangle sharp in the quiet night. He glanced back, lips quirking. "You good, Tattoo?"

Cherry nodded, throat tight. "Yeah. Yeah, man. Solid." The lie burned and left his gut a tangle of want and nerves, but he'd be damned if he let it show. He'd faced down far bigger threats than this. So many times. In a war-torn countryside, barroom brawls, brothers gone rogue, and even the endless grind of keeping the IMC's Baton Rouge chapter in line. This? This was just a man, a beer, and it was simply one night. Except it wasn't. It was everything he'd buried for so many years, the emotion and anticipation finally clawing its way free.

The door swung open, spilling warm light onto the porch, and Suit Guy stepped aside with a mock bow. "After you, gorgeous." Cherry snorted, brushing past, their shoulders grazing just enough to spark another wave of heat up his arm. Inside, the place was simple but lived-in with dark wood floors, a smart leather couch, a bowed window seat tucked in one corner. A framed photo on the wall caught his eye: Suit Guy in a sharp suit, arm around an older woman with a grin that matched his own. Family, maybe. Roots and ties that Cherry didn't let himself linger on too often.

"Beer?" Suit Guy was already at the fridge, pulling two bottles, the clink of glass a tether bringing Cherry back to the moment.

"Yeah, hit me." He took the offered bottle, cold and sweating against his palm, and popped the cap with a twist of his wrist. The first swig went down sharp and bitter, the hops scent helping ground him. He leaned against the counter, watching Suit Guy mirror him on one side, hip cocked, eyes steady.

"So," Suit Guy started, voice low, "you said you're green. First time out?"

Cherry's laugh was rough, half-caught in his chest. "First time *here*, yeah. Not my usual haunt." He took another pull, letting the silence stretch, then met those eyes head-on. "Been thinking about it a long damn time, though. Too long."

Suit Guy's gaze softened, just a flicker, but it hit Cherry like a punch. "Takes guts, man. Owning it. Acting on it." He tipped his bottle in a quiet toast. "Respect."

Cherry clinked his bottle against it, the sound sharp in the stillness. "Guts or stupidity. Jury's still out." He smirked, but it dropped quickly. His free hand drifted to his chest, ghosting over where his vest would've sat, the weight of his colors a phantom ache. "Got a lot riding on keeping things tight, you know? Where I'm from, this"—he gestured between them—"ain't exactly standard issue. There's understanding in my circle, I've made sure of that. But I've held my silence about myself."

"Fuck standard," Suit Guy said, grin flashing. "You're here now. That's what counts." He stepped closer, bottle dangling from his fingers, close enough that Cherry caught the faint spice of an earthy cologne over the beer. "And for the record, you're doing fine so far."

Cherry's breath hitched, but he held his ground, letting the tension coil tighter. "Yeah?

We'll see." He tipped his head back for another swig, throat working, aware of those eyes intently tracking every move.

***

Denis

Denis watched Tattoo, the guy still had no name, but damn if the moniker didn't suit him, down that beer like it was a lifeline, and fuck, the man made every moment look good. The way his Adam's apple bobbed, the flex of ink-wrapped muscle under the dim kitchen light was a show, intentional or not, and Denis was his willing and eager audience. He took off the suit jacket and tossed it to the surface behind him, then leaned back, elbows on the counter, letting the moment simmer. *No rush. Not yet.*

He'd clocked the nerves the second they'd hit the sidewalk. Tattoo's tightening shoulders, the flicker of hesitation in his gray eyes. "Green," he'd said, and Denis believed it. Not wet-behind-the-ears green, though. Public green. Lack of opportunity meant this guy carried something weighty, a hardness that said he'd seen shit, bested it, and survived it. The kind of man Denis usually found in courtrooms, not clubs, all swagger and scars with everything soft buried deep.

"You're staring again, Suit Guy," Tattoo said, voice rough-edged, breaking the quiet. He set his bottle down, empty, and crossed his arms, tattoos shifting with the flex.

"Caught me." Denis grinned, unrepentant, and took a slow sip of his own beer. "You're worth it." He let his eyes roam over every part on display, Tattoo's chest, arms, that jawline begging for teeth. The man didn't flinch, just held his gaze, steady as stone. *Good.* Denis liked a challenge.

"Flattery'll get you to all the places," Tattoo shot back, a smirk tugging his lips. "What's your story, then? You don't strike me as green."

Denis chuckled, rolling the bottle between his palms. "Not green, no. Been around this block a few times. I'm a lawyer. These days in the private sector. Days are long, and even in my own practice the cases are shit half the time. But, at the end of the day, I'm damn good at my job." He shrugged, casual, but pride laced the words. "Today was a win, though. The good guys triumphed, my client walked, and I needed this."

He gestured vaguely...club, beer, Tattoo...as if it explained everything.

Tattoo's brows lifted, impressed or surprised, hard to tell. "Lawyer, huh? Didn't peg you for a legal eagle." He nodded at Denis' shirt, unbuttoned just enough to ditch the polish. "Guess you can shed the suit easy enough."

"Gotta breathe sometime." Denis stepped closer, closing the gap, voice dropping low. "You shedding anything tonight, Tattoo?"

The air thickened, charged, and Tattoo's smirk faltered, replaced by something hungrier. "Maybe. Depends on you, big guy." He straightened, squaring off with him, and Denis felt the shift, Tattoo's nerves giving way to heat, a dare in those storm-gray eyes.

Denis set his beer aside, slow and deliberate, and leaned in, hands braced on the counter either side of Tattoo's hips. Not touching, not yet, just close enough to feel the warmth radiating off him. "I'm game," he murmured, lips brushing the shell of Tattoo's ear. "You?"

***

Cherry

Cherry's pulse kicked up, Suit Guy's breath was hot against his ear, and for a second, he froze. Not from fear. *Nope, because fuck that noise.* But from the sheer headiness of it, the knowledge of the line he was about to cross. Then Suit Guy's hands slid to his waist, firm and sure, and the freeze melted into a slow burn. Cherry tilted his head, meeting those dark eyes, and nodded once, sharp. "Yeah. I'm all in."

The words barely hit the air before Suit Guy's mouth was on his, hard and claiming, picking up where they'd left off. Cherry surged into it, hands fisting in that damn shirt, pulling him closer. Tongues clashed, beer and want mixing on his tastebuds, and he groaned, low and rough, the sound swallowed by the kiss. Suit Guy's fingers dug into his hips, tugging him off the counter, and Cherry went willingly, boots scuffing the floor as they stumbled towards the couch.

They hit it in a tangle, Cherry's back against the leather, Suit Guy looming over him, one knee braced between his thighs. The weight was good. Exactly the kind of solid and real detail needed to settle him in the moment. Cherry gave in and arched up, hips chasing more. Suit Guy grinned against his mouth before kissing him hard, then pulled back, breath ragged. "Fuck, you're hot," the man muttered, hands sliding under Cherry's shirt, rucking it up to bare ink and muscle.

Cherry laughed, breathless, and yanked at Suit Guy's shirt in return. "Back at you, asshole." Buttons popped, fabric parted, and then it was skin on skin, heat searing through him. He dragged his nails down Suit Guy's back, earning a hiss and a harder grind of hips, cocks rubbing through denim. Too much, but still not enough. *Need more.* Cherry's head spun, every touch lighting him up like a live wire.

"Name," Suit Guy panted, lips trailing down Cherry's neck, teeth scraping. "Gimme something to call you."

"Cherry." It slipped out, his road name, not government, and he didn't care. *It feels right for here and now.* "You?"

"I'm Denis. Hi, Cherry. Good to meet you." A nip at his collarbone, then a hot mouth moved against his skin. There was humor in the man's voice. "Fits you. Cherry. You taste sweet as one."

"Shut up and kiss me," Cherry growled, hauling Denis down, and the world narrowed again to those lips, the wandering hands, and the creak of leather under them. Outside, the city hummed, oblivious, but in here, it was just them, burning through the night.

***

Later, it could have been minutes or hours, Cherry was sprawled on the couch, shirt gone, jeans half-unzipped, Denis a warm weight slumped against him. The beer buzz had faded, replaced by a different high, one carved out of shared gasps and the ache of new bruises. He stared at the ceiling, chest heaving, gaze tracing tiny cracks in the plaster like they'd map where this was going.

Denis shifted, propping an elbow to look down at him, hair mussed and eyes lazy. "You good, Cherry?"

"Yeah." He was. Way better than good, alive in a way he hadn't felt in years. *Maybe ever.* The rushed grind had still been more satisfying than anything else he'd ever experienced. A sudden stab of concern made his breath catch. "Fuck yeah. You?"

"Fucking great." Denis smirked, brushing a thumb over Cherry's jaw, lingering on the stubble. "Worth every second of that dancefloor tease."

Cherry snorted, shoving at him half-hearted. "Tease, huh? Who jumped who?"

"Mutual jumping," Denis countered, leaning in for a lazy kiss, softer this time, less frantic. Cherry sank into it, letting the edge bleed out, replaced by something steadier.

When they broke apart, Denis rolled off, and grabbed a couple sections of paper towel from the kitchen, handing over half even as he worked to mop up his abs. Cherry went at it more slowly, gaze locked on every movement the man made. Denis made his way back into the kitchen, grabbing more beers from the fridge and came back to the couch, handing one over. Cherry took it, sitting up, the cool bottle a shock against his overheated skin. "So," he said, voice gravelly, "this a one-off, or...?"

Denis paused, mid-sip, then met his eyes, serious for once. "Up to you, man. I'm not running. You?"

Cherry thought of the club, the vest folded back home, the life he'd built. Then this, the feeling of being with Denis, the night, the taste of freedom, the sensation of setting his own course. "Not running," he said finally, clinking his bottle against Denis'. "Let's see where it rides."

***

Denis

Denis watched Cherry sip that beer, the bottle tilting just enough to catch the dim light of the living room, casting a faint sheen across the ink that snaked up his arms. He'd identified tangled designs of skulls, chains, and something Denis couldn't quite make out, faded with time. He sat sprawled on the couch, leather jacket slung over the armrest, all edges and muscle, like he'd been carved from mountain granite. He belonged there, somehow, in a way Denis couldn't explain, and something twisted in his chest. It was sharp, unfamiliar, a pang that wasn't lust but wasn't *not* lust either.

They'd both just come, sweat still hot on their skin, so it wasn't a misplaced urgency. Even though things had happened similar to so many meaningless encounters, because hell yeah, he'd had hookups before, plenty of them. Always quick, transactional, a blur of bodies in dimly lit rooms. But this? *This was different.* Cherry wasn't just a body, wasn't just a release. *Different even from the single time he'd attempted a relationship before. Big fail there, Ricardo hadn't understood the nuance of "exclusive."* There was a story with Cherry that intrigued, etched into every scar and tattoo, a history Denis wanted to unravel, patch by patch, as if he were peeling back the layers of a case he couldn't leave unsolved.

"You're staring again," Cherry said, his voice rough around the edges, a drawl laced with something softer. He smirked, but his storm-gray eyes were a little less guarded now, the steel wall he'd walked in with starting to crack.

"Habit," Denis replied, grinning as he settled beside him, their shoulders brushing. The contact was deliberate but light, a test. "You're still worth it." He nudged Cherry's knee with his own, feeling the solid weight of him, the way he didn't flinch or pull away. "That 'ride' comment earlier, you got a bike stashed somewhere?"

Cherry's laugh was low, warm, rumbling up from his chest like an engine kicking to life. "Yeah. Big bastard too, full custom paint job, got it done in blue like the IMC wings." Pride flickered in his voice, sharp and bright, and Denis filed it away. *IMC, huh?* Incoherent Motorcycle Club, had to be. *It fits.* The ink, the scars, the way Cherry carried himself like he could take a punch and give two back, all spoke of a life lived hard and loud. Former military, too, Denis guessed, catching the hint of command in the way Cherry's shoulders squared even at rest. Decades of discipline under all that chaos.

"Gonna show me sometime?" Denis asked, aiming for casual, but the words came out heavier than he'd intended. He surprised himself with how much he meant it. Being with Cherry on a bike, wind tearing past, him riding bitch just to feel it, to press himself against that broad back and let the world blur away. The intensity of the image hit him square in the chest, a rush of want he hadn't expected.

"Maybe." Cherry's gaze slid sideways, assessing, those storm-gray eyes catching Denis's and holding them for a beat before he grinned dangerously. "You'd look good on it."

"Damn right I would." Denis laughed, and the tension between them eased, settling into something comfortable, dangerous in its own way, similar to the quiet before the readout of a verdict. He leaned back, arm stretching along the couch behind Cherry, not touching but close enough to feel the heat radiating off him. "Stick around, Cherry. I've got more beer, and I'm not done with you yet."

Cherry's smirk was slow, deliberate, a flash of teeth that sent a shiver down Denis's spine. "Good. 'Cause I'm not done either." He set the beer on the coffee table, the clink of glass on wood punctuating the moment, and turned his body just enough to face Denis more fully. His knee pressed against Denis's thigh now, a steady, grounding weight.

Denis held his gaze, letting the silence stretch, thick with unspoken things. He could see the understanding now, the flicker of hesitation in Cherry's eyes, the way his fingers flexed against his own knee like he was bracing for something. This wasn't just another night for him either. Denis had caught the way Cherry had stiffened earlier, when their hands brushed reaching for the same bottle, the way his breath had hitched before he'd covered it with a laugh.

First time with a man, Denis realized, the pieces clicking into place, and in the moment, Cherry had lost the sense of hesitation. If he'd been military during Don't Ask, Don't Tell, well, it meant he'd likely been closeted for decades, carrying that weight alone. No wonder he'd been all sharp edges when he'd walked in, like a man expecting a fight.

"You don't have to—" Denis started, voice softer now, giving him an out, but Cherry cut him off with a shake of his head.

"Don't." Cherry's tone was firm, but not harsh. "I'm here 'cause I want to be." He leaned in, just a fraction, his breath warm against Denis's jaw. "Been a long time comin', that's all."

Denis swallowed, his pulse kicking up. "Yeah?"

"Yeah." Cherry's hand moved then, tentative at first, resting on Denis's thigh. It was big, calloused, with a biker's grip that tightened slightly as he found his nerve. "Gotta say, you're makin' it real easy, lawyer man."

"Denis," he corrected, voice rougher than he meant it to be. "And you're not so bad yourself, Cherry." He tilted his head, closing the distance until their lips were a breath apart, waiting, letting Cherry decide.

Cherry's exhale was shaky, but he didn't pull back. "Fuck it," he muttered, and then he kissed him. It was hard, hungry, a dam breaking. It was all heat at first, more decades of pent-up want crashing through, but Denis met him there, hand sliding to the back of Cherry's neck, settling him. The kiss softened after a moment, turned searching, and Cherry groaned low in his throat, a sound that vibrated through Denis's chest.

When they broke apart, Cherry's forehead rested against his, both of them breathing hard. "Didn't think it'd feel like this," Cherry admitted, voice raw, unguarded in a way that made Denis's heart stutter.

"Like what?" Denis asked, thumb brushing along the stubble of Cherry's jaw.

"Like I found something I've been missin' my whole damn life." Cherry pulled back just enough to meet his eyes, and the vulnerability there, the depth of his trust, hit Denis harder than the kiss had.

He grinned, leaning in to steal another quick press of lips. "Good thing I've got nowhere to be. We've got time to figure it out."

Cherry's laugh was quieter this time, but real, and he settled back against the couch, his hand still on Denis's thigh, possessive now. "Yeah. Guess we do."

Chapter Four

Cherry

The ride back to his place was a blur with streetlights streaking past like tracer rounds, the stale air inside the rideshare pressing against his skin.

Cherry slumped in the backseat, boots braced wide on the floorboard, staring out at the Baton Rouge night as it smeared into shadows. His chest still hummed, a live wire buzzing under his ribs, but the farther he got from Denis' apartment, the more it felt like a dream slipping through his fingers. *Unreal.* He was off kilter, even sitting in the car seat was a chore. Like he'd stepped out of his own skin for a night and now couldn't find the way back in.

He gave the driver a gruff "thanks" as he tapped the tip button and hauled himself out. Cherry stood on the cracked asphalt of his driveway, the familiar bulk of his bike in the open garage gleaming under the sodium glow of a streetlamp. Home. His sanctuary was two stories of weathered brick and secrets, bought with cash from a decade of enforcing the IMC's will. The door from the garage to the kitchen groaned as he shouldered it open, the dark swallowing him whole until he flicked the kitchen light. It buzzed to life, harsh and yellow, casting jagged shadows across the room.

Cherry shed his boots by the door, the thud of leather on tile familiar and grounding, and crossed to the fridge. Beer in hand, he didn't bother with a glass, just tipped the can back, letting the cold bite chase the lingering taste of Denis from his tongue. *Denis. Suit Guy.* A man with that grin, those hands, and the way he'd pulled Cherry apart and pieced him back together in the span of a few hours. He set the beer down hard, metal clinking against the counter, and dragged a hand over his face, stubble rasping under his palm.

"What the fuck was that?" he muttered, the soft question swallowed by the empty house. Beer in hand he paced to the living room, dropping onto the couch which was a beast of cracked leather that sagged under his weight. His vest flowed through his mind, patches stark against the black, watching him as if it were a jury. *Cherry. Enforcer. Semper Fi.* The man he'd built, brick by brick, over decades of blood and loyalty to the two entities. And yet, last night, he'd been someone else. Someone raw, unguarded, chasing a hunger he'd buried so deep and for so long he'd nearly forgotten its shape.

He fished his phone from his pocket, thumb hovering over the screen. Denis' number glowed there, punched in before he'd left. It was either a lifeline or a landmine, he couldn't tell which. *Call him. Just fucking call him.* His pulse thumped, too loud again, and he scrolled the contact screen up and down, finger twitching closer to the "Call" button with each scroll. What would he even say? *Hey, Suit Guy, I'm losing my damn mind over here. Wanna tell me it was real?* Pathetic. He locked the screen, tossed the phone onto the cushion beside him, and leaned back, staring at the ceiling.

The certainty he'd felt when they'd been chest to chest, Denis' breath hot against his neck, was fraying, threads pulling loose with every tick of the clock. Maybe it was a fluke. A one-off. Maybe he'd imagined the way Denis looked at him, like he saw past the ink, the gruffness, and the growl to something worth keeping. Cherry snorted, bitter, and lifted the beer again, draining it. He'd faced down worse than doubt. No matter fists, knives, even the weight of a brother's betrayal. This shouldn't shake him.

But it did. Throughout the next early morning hours there were eleven times he picked up the phone, thumb nearly brushing the call button, heart slamming against his ribs. Eleven times he stopped, tossing it back down, cursing himself for a coward. The twelfth time the siren called, he stood, shoved it into a pocket, grabbed his vest, yanked his boots back on, and stormed out to the garage instead. The bike roared to life under him, a snarl of power that drowned out the noise in his head. He peeled out into the night, wind tearing at him, chasing the road until the uncertainty blurred into the brightening horizon. But Denis stayed, a ghost riding shotgun, and Cherry couldn't shake him loose.

His two oaths complimented each other. One to the US Constitution, and one to the club. Both were supported by the bones of those who had come before. Cherry blinked his stinging eyes and slowed the bike, shocked he'd been riding in excess of...well, of everything, lucky to be doing so without having a red and blue escort. Busk would have his ass if he'd pulled so much as a ticket while doing something so incredibly stupid. *If he knew about Denis, he might grant me some slack.* Cherry shook his head, rattling the helmet around on his skull. "He'd be right to give me a beatdown, if anything had happened." He knew that deep inside the chapter VP's heart was a sweet and sappy "love will find a way" theory. No matter how rough and gruff he acted.

The first time he'd met Busk was at a bike washing fundraiser years ago. Cherry had ridden past, eyeballing the women in skimpy outfits caressing each piece of chrome with a sudsy rag, thinking he could pay for a wash and dry. That would cut down on the bullshit tasks he needed to finish up before he could feel comfortable roaring out of town, letting the turns of the road dictate his journey.

Decided, he'd rolled around the corner and circled the block until he was back in front of the bike wash. Easing to a stop, Cherry lifted a requesting finger to a young lady approaching with a clipboard in hand. One wash, one dry. A tall wall of a man interrupted her, thick fingers plucking the clipboard and pen with a deftness that belied the sheer size of the man.

"Busk." Hand extended to Cherry, the man had looked him up and down.

"Pleased. I'm Cherry." Giving his military call sign in that moment had felt right. After all, he'd been Cherry for more years than he'd like to admit.

Chapter Five
Denis

Denis shoved the file across his desk, papers spilling in a riot of chaos, and leaned back in his chair, the springs creaking under him. It was way too early on a Monday morning, and the scant staff already in the office hummed around him, same as always. The pro bono case in front of him was a skeleton, bones picked clean. This was just a kid caught with a dime bag and a non-existent rap sheet that didn't match the scared-shitless face Denis had seen in lockup. Thin folder, thinner story. Something stank, and it wasn't just the precinct's shitty plumbing.

He tapped a pen against his teeth, then grabbed his phone, punching in a number from memory. "Ricky," he said when the line picked up, voice clipped. "Got a job. Kid named Marcus Warner, nineteen, picked up on possession. His grandmother wanted to hire me, but they're tight on money so it's pro bono. But the file's light, too light. Follow and watch, yeah? Dig me something I can use."

"On it, boss," came the reply, rough as gravel, and the call dropped. Ricky Parrado was a bloodhound, a PI who'd sniffed out more dirt for Denis than half the cops in Baton Rouge combined. If there was a thread to pull, he'd find it. Denis tossed the phone down and flipped to the next file. It was a domestic, and messy, the kind that made his skin crawl while his bank balance sighed with happiness, but his focus splintered yet another time, dragged back to Saturday night like a moth to a flame.

Cherry. That name, that voice, so low and ragged, like it'd been scraped over asphalt, and it lived rent-free in his skull. The biker vibe should have screamed trouble. Hell, all that ink that told a story Denis hadn't cracked yet, the multitude of scars that hinted at a life spent swinging at enemies, those storm-gray eyes flashing vulnerable one second, hard as steel the next. And that body. Jesus fuck, the way Cherry had moved against him, all power and need, grinding into him until they could burn the world down together. Denis shifted in his seat, pants tightening at the memory, and forced his eyes back to the file. *Focus, asshole.*

But Cherry wouldn't leave. Denis saw him in the margins of every page. The illusion of those thick forearms flexing as he gripped Denis' neck, the hitch in his breath when they'd kissed, the way he'd said "not running" like it was a vow. Denis had fucked plenty of guys, blown off steam in dark corners or between sweaty sheets, but none had stuck in his head like this. Cherry was a puzzle, a contradiction, a roughneck biker with a soft underbelly, green but not fragile, hiding something big behind that steely glare.

He scribbled a note for one of his junior associates on the domestic case, then tossed the pen, leaning back to stare at the ceiling. The biker angle gnawed at him. The motorcycle club, IMC no question, but Baton Rouge had its share of other players. He'd defended a few over the years, patched-up outlaws with more loyalty than sense. Cherry fit the mold but also didn't. He was too steady, too real. Denis wanted to peel him open, layer by layer, and see what made him tick.

His phone buzzed, Ricky, probably, and he snatched it up, grateful for the distraction. "Yeah?"

"Preliminary on Warner," Ricky said, voice crackling. "Kid's a runner. Just small-time, but connected. Got eyes on him now. Give me a week."

"Good. Keep me posted." Denis hung up, but his mind was already drifting again, back to Cherry sprawled on his couch, chest heaving, that slow smirk promising more. He groaned, scrubbing a hand over his face. "Get your shit together, Chapin." But the truth settled heavily that Cherry wasn't just in his head, he was under his skin, and Denis wasn't sure he wanted him out.

Chapter Six

Cherry

The Baton Rouge clubhouse smelled as it always did, a biker's mix of motor oil, stale beer, and the faint tang of weed. Cherry leaned against the bar, one boot hooked on the rail, slowly sipping from a lukewarm bottle as prospects hustled around through mid-afternoon streaks of sunlight, wiping down tables and hauling chairs into rows. A couple of patched members, Rook and T-Bone, lounged nearby, shooting the shit about a run over to Gulfport that'd gone sideways. Cherry half-listened, nodding when it mattered, his mind still tangled up in the ghost of Denis' hands, the echo of that night.

"Prospects are green as hell," Rook muttered, jerking his chin at a skinny kid fumbling a stack of folding chairs. "Gonna be a long fuckin' night for the meeting if they don't shape up."

"Mother'll whip 'em straight," T-Bone said, grinning around a toothpick. "Always does."

Cherry snorted, setting his beer down. "Yeah, well, VP wants it perfect. Big dogs coming in, gotta show 'em Baton Rouge ain't slacking. Prez is pushin' VP, and he's pushin' us. Gotta make the cut. Ruger and Busk are gonna be looking for anything out of line." He pushed off the bar, rolling his shoulders. "C'mon, let's get the back room sorted." He tapped the side of his nose. "Never know when Mother is looking around. Anyone seen Pony today?" The men laughed as they followed him. Pony was IMC's resident IT guru, based in Hammond.

They filed into the meeting space within the clubhouse, which was a low-ceilinged box with a long table scarred from years of fists and bottles. Cherry hauled a pair of chairs from the corner, Rook grabbed a broom, and T-Bone started pinning the IMC bylaws up on the wall, the paper yellowed but sacred. The rhythm was easy, familiar, more muscle memory from a hundred setups like this. Cherry let it steady him, the whisk of the broom and rustle of paper drowning out the noise in his head.

He was giving the table a final wipe when Rook's phone buzzed, sharp and insistent. The man frowned, answered, and went still. "Fuck. Yeah, on it." He hung up, eyes cutting to Cherry. "That was Busk. Diesel's down. Highway 10, some cage clipped him. He's alive, but it don't sound real good."

Cherry's gut clenched, the rag dropping from his hand. "Let's roll." They picked up a few more members as they made their way through the clubhouse. Cherry sent a text to the officers' group, watched long enough to see his president was informed, and then shoved the phone deep in his pocket. "Stay out of the back room," he told the one probationary member. "Keep the prospects out of it, too." They'd be leaving the clubhouse with scant protection, but he believed the men in the vests sporting any version of affiliation with IMC would defend to the death.

Ten minutes later, six bikes roared onto the scene, engines snarling as they pulled up to a mess of flashing lights and twisted metal. Diesel's ride, a matte-black beauty, was a mangled heap on the shoulder, front wheel bent like a pretzel. The man himself was propped against a guardrail, one arm cradled awkward and bloody, face pale but he was cursing up a storm as a paramedic worked on him. Cherry swung off his bike, boots crunching gravel, and clocked the cops milling around. There were three of 'em, tense, hands hovering near holsters.

"He good?" Cherry called to the VP, Busk, who was kneeling by Diesel.

"Arm's fucked, but he'll live," Busk growled, standing. "Cage didn't even stop. Motherfucker just peeled out."

Cherry nodded, relief warring with the adrenaline pumping through him. He turned to check the bike from closer, but a shadow loomed up. It was some rookie cop, barely old enough to shave, chest puffed out like a goddamn peacock.

"Back off," the kid barked, stepping into Cherry's space, voice cracking with nerves. "This ain't your scene."

Cherry's jaw tightened, but he kept his tone level, hands loose at his sides. "Brother's down, kid. Just checking on him."

"Don't 'kid' me," the cop snapped, finger jabbing too close to Cherry's chest. "You bikers think you own the road? Step back, or I'll—"

"Or you'll what?" Cherry cut in, voice dropping low, the enforcer's edge bleeding through. He didn't move, didn't flinch, just stared the rookie down, gray eyes hard as flint. The air thickened, one of the other cops turned, hands twitching. Busk stepped up, a wall of leather and calm, but it was too late. The rookie's pride was stung, and he grabbed Cherry's arm, yanking like he could muscle him anywhere.

"Hands off," Cherry growled, shaking him loose, but the kid was already shouting for backup, and next thing he knew, he was face-first against a cruiser, wrists pinned.

"Arresting you for interfering," the rookie spat, breathless with his own bullshit.

"For what?" Cherry roared as the door slammed shut, locking him in the backseat. He twisted, glaring through the glass as Busk argued with the cop, pointing at his bike. "Impound," he caught through the muffled yelling, and his stomach dropped. "Get someone to ride it home," he shouted, but the rookie cut him off with a sneer, "Evidence, asshole," and Busk threw up his hands, done.

Cherry slumped back, watching the ambulance pull out, ferrying Diesel to the nearest bone doctor. Busk held a phone to his ear, then shouted, "Lawyer's tied up with Mother chapter bullshit so sit tight, Prez is on it. Ruger says we'll get you out, you know we'll get you out, brother."

Cherry nodded, forcing his breathing to slow. "At least I'm not cuffed," he muttered, bitter, as the engine growled to life and the cruiser rolled towards the station.

Chapter Seven

Denis

Denis' office was a war zone of discarded coffee cups, careless coffee rings bleeding into each other across papers littering his desk like a topographic map of exhaustion. He tapped his laptop, refreshing his inbox for the tenth time in as many minutes. Still no word from Ricky. The Marcus Warner case was a ghost. Still way too thin, too quiet, and the clock was ticking. He sighed, dragging a hand through his hair, and opened his chat with Carole.

Need an extension on Warner, he typed, cursor hovering over send. Before he could hit it, the screen pulsed that godawful lime green, Carole's pick because she swore it kept her sharp, and her preemptive reply popped up: *Already filed for an extension for Warner, boss.*

Denis barked a laugh, shaking his head. "Of course you did." Another pulse, and: *PI meeting set for tomorrow, 10 a.m. Don't be late.* He grinned, leaning back in his chair. Carole Morris was a force of nature, fifty-something, sharp as a tack, and the only reason his life didn't collapse under the weight of case files and burned coffee. Call her a secretary, and she'd gladly gut you with a smile. His aunt, she was also the only person in his family he was close to.

He was still chuckling when his gaze drifted, mind rolling unbidden to the memory of Cherry sprawled on his couch, ink gleaming under the light, that rough laugh rumbling through Denis' bones. The man was a goddamn magnet, pulling Denis' focus no matter how deep he buried himself in work. He'd replayed that night a hundred times. Going from their time on the dancefloor, the kiss, to the way Cherry's voice cracked with want. That slow, wanton grind. *Jesus God.* Green, he'd said, but there was nothing fragile about him. Just layers Denis itched to peel back.

His phone buzzed, snapping him out of it. He grabbed it, hoping for Ricky, but it was just a spam text. "Fuck," he muttered, tossing it down. He needed that report. It would give him something to sink his teeth into, something to keep Cherry from hijacking every spare thought. Because right now, the biker was winning, and Denis wasn't sure he minded.

Chapter Eight

Cherry

The cruiser carried memories of stale sweat and cheap vinyl, the backseat felt sticky under Cherry's jeans as they rolled into the station. The cop up front was not the rookie. He was older and calm when he glanced back in the mirror. "You good back there?"

"What do you think?" Cherry shot back, then bit his tongue, forcing a shrug. "Sorry. Yeah, I'm okay. You know what I'm being held for?"

"Nope. I'm just your ride to the shop." The cop's tone was flat, uninterested, and Cherry let it drop, staring out at the blur of neon and concrete.

They booked him quickly, prints, mugshot, the whole dance, and shoved him into a holding cell with a bench and a dented steel toilet. He paced for a while, boots echoing, then sank down, elbows on his knees, head in his hands. The rookie's bullshit charge wouldn't stick. And he knew Busk would call the club's lawyer, some slick bastard out of Hammond, but it was his bike being impounded that gnawed at him. That baby was his soul, blue paint chipped from a thousand miles of road grit, every dent a story. Losing it to a tow lot over this? Fuck that.

He replayed the scene, remembering Diesel's blood on the gravel, the rookie cop's shaky bravado, Busk's helpless shrug. *Arm busted but breathing*, he told himself about Diesel. *Better than a slab*. Still, the anger simmered, low and steady, mixing with the ache of already missing his ride. And under it all, Denis flickered, those dark eyes, that grin. Cherry snorted, shaking his head. Locked up, and he was still mooning like a damn teenager.

Chapter Nine

Denis

Denis slumped in his chair, eyes burning as he closed them, the day's weight pressing down like a physical thing. Case files blurred together, but memories of Cherry stayed sharp. His tattooed arms, that low growl of a voice, the way he'd arched into Denis like he'd been starving for it. *Perfect. So perfect.* Every box ticked with a sharp and bold mark, because he was gorgeous, sharp, funny, and came with an edge to him that cut just right. Denis smiled into the dark, letting the images play.

The phone shrilled, shattering the quiet. He blinked at the wall clock reading 9:47 p.m., and grabbed the phone. Carole's name flashed. They should have both been gone long ago. "Yes, ma'am?" he said, hitting speaker.

"Denis, Judge Cooper's on line two. Wants you to reprise your old role as public defender." Her voice was crisp and no-nonsense, even this late.

He frowned. "I'm not...never mind. Okay, I'll take it." Not his usual gig these days, not when the private practice he'd built up with sweat and blood paid way better, but Cooper was a friend from his public defender beginnings. He tapped the blinking line. "Judge Cooper, great to hear from you. What brings you slumming in my neighborhood?"

"Denis." The judge's drawl was warm, laced with a chuckle. "You know I told you to call me Daylon."

"Alright, Daylon, how you holding up?"

"Funny you should ask. I need someone I know. Someone I can trust. My normal PD is out, the man had some family emergency, but there's a guy in lockup I want bonded out ASAP. His lawyer's AWOL."

Denis leaned forwards, interest piqued. "What's the charge?"

"Stupid one, but you didn't hear that from me. Rookie got his feathers ruffled, overreacted. Bullshit resisting charge. I'd cut him loose on his own, but protocol's protocol, and next year's an election year."

"Bond set?"

"Need you to handle it. Can you be here by 10:30 tonight?"

Denis glanced at the clock. The timeline was tight, but doable. "Oh, night court. Fun times. Yeah, I'm in. Who's the lucky bastard?"

"Tom Palant. IMC guy. You'll see the file."

Denis froze, a jolt running through him. *Could it be Cherry?* "Got it," he said, voice steady despite the rapid thud of his pulse. "See you soon."

***

Cherry

The cell was a windowless concrete box, where the kind of quiet pressed in until your own breathing sounded loud. He was almost sorry he didn't have any company. Cherry sat as he had for several hours, head tipped back against the chilly wall, eyes half-closed, figuring he was stuck in holding till morning. Then boots clomped down the hall, and a voice barked, "Palant. Courtroom. Let's go."

He straightened, squinting. "It's late."

"Tell me something I didn't know. What? You got somewhere else to be?" The jailer grinned, clearly amused, and swung the door wide. "Come on."

Cherry stood, backing up with wrists crossed, a remembered habit from long ago rougher days, but the guy waved him off. "Naw, no cuffs. IMC's got my respect, man. Y'all fixed my Auntie Joan's roof out in Slidell few years back. She'd never ask, but after the 'cane you all just showed up and took care of her. I ain't forgetting that."

Cherry blinked as he turned, surprised, and stepped out as instructed. "Thank you." The hallway stretched ahead, fluorescent lights buzzing, and he followed, boots heavy. Court this late meant someone pulled strings, Busk, maybe, or the lawyer finally waking up. He didn't dare hope for more.

*****

Denis

Denis paced the defender's room, a claustrophobic closet of chipped paint and flickering light, flipping through the slim folder they'd handed him at the courthouse door. *Tom Palant, 49, Marine vet, mechanic, IMC Baton Rouge.* No priors worth a damn, a few drunk and disorderly from decades ago. And the rookie's flimsy charge from today. *Resisting, my ass.* He was scanning for an alias, something to tie it to Cherry when the door creaked open.

He turned, and there he was—Cherry, in the flesh, all ink and striking storm-gray eyes, rocking back on his heels as if he'd been gut-punched. Denis' heart kicked, but he played it cool, striding over with a hand out. "Hi."

"Hi," Cherry echoed, taking it slow, their palms sliding together a beat too long. Warm, rough, familiar.

"Good to see you," Denis said, pumping twice before letting go.

"You too. Sorry to drag you out so late." Cherry's voice was steady, but his eyes flickered with surprise, maybe relief.

"When Judge Cooper calls, I answer. He couldn't sort your rep, so he tapped me." Denis shut the door behind the jailer, gesturing to a chair. "Sit, Cherry." He paused, grinning. "Hmmm. Nope. Can't bring myself to call you Tom. Simply doesn't fit."

Cherry's smile was small, but real. "Haven't been Tom in forever, man. You've got the real me."

***

Cherry

The fuck? Cherry stared at Denis, the man he'd connected with on a raw level, and had been fighting to forget. The man now standing there in a rumpled shirt and a grin that could smack the sense out of him. Lawyer, yeah, he'd said that, but public defender? He was sure Denis had said he was in private practice, which made way more sense. Denis was private money, not living off county scraps. Cherry rocked back, caught off guard, but the memory of Denis' hand in his grounded him, that slow slide of skin saying *we're not strangers*. Okay. He'd roll with it.

He hooked a boot around the chair, swinging it to straddle the seat, arms crossed over the back. Denis sat too, close enough to feel, and Cherry let himself breathe. There was still the trouble he'd landed in, and his bike was still in impound, but just having Denis here, no matter what questions it raised, felt like a stable line back to good.

Denis nodded brusquely, and Cherry had to remind himself of the lawyer/client relationship when he swallowed as if his throat was tight. Denis said, "It matters to me, thanks." They both pulled in a silent breath before Denis continued, "So, tell me what happened."

Cherry pointed at the folder. "You've got the gist." He let his smile grow again, Denis seemingly unable to look away. "You gonna stay way over there?"

"Hell no, but first we have business to take care of," Denis shot back, before sliding his chair closer. "Judge wants this gone, I don't know why, just that he's itching to cut you loose. Start at the accident, walk me through."

Denis's gaze held his, steady and deep, and Cherry knew, deep in his gut, this wasn't just a favor anymore. It was personal.

"What judge?" Cherry wracked his memory trying to remember the name spoken of in locked rooms, a man who felt like he owed the IMC. Much like the jailer earlier did over the assistance given to a family member. "Cooper?" He knew he'd hit paydirt as soon as Denis's eyes widened ever so slightly.

"Yeah, Cooper." Denis confirmed. "How do you know him?"

Cherry shot a glance at the door, then up at the light and held a finger to his lips. He stood, suddenly about ninety percent sure there was a recording device in the room. He wanted to confirm or disprove that before they continued the conversation they needed to have. "Oh, I know a lotta people." He kept his voice steady as he knelt to look underneath the table. Nothing there. When he picked his head up, Denis was staring at him, head cocked inquisitively to one side.

"I bet you do." Denis's immediate understanding of the task at hand made Cherry weirdly proud and he grinned broadly at the man. "Like me. I know you and you know me."

"Yes, I do." Cherry pulled his chair over underneath the old fashioned overhead light assembly and clambered to stand on the seat. Balancing himself against the ceiling, he rose to his toes and found himself in front of a tape recorder. Staring at the wiring set-up, he motioned Denis to turn off the switch at the wall. The red light on the recorder went out immediately. *Good deal, I don't have to mess with it.*

He climbed down off the chair as he gave Denis a nod. "Recorder up there, wired into the light so it only has power as long as the light is on. No light, no power." He made a poof-motion with one hand. "I can't imagine they'd have two devices, so I expect we're safe to talk about everything now."

Denis's chin rose, brow furrowed. "There's a recorder in this room? In the public defender's room? That's illegal."

Cherry fought a laugh and Denis glared at him.

"You might think you're hiding your thoughts, but I can assure you that your face is telling me the whole story." Denis grumbled as he leaned back in his chair. "I mean, it's not as if I haven't stretched the definition of legal before, but this is blatant and just wrong."

"You can tell Judge Cooper you found it, and watch his face. Betcha he knows all about it." Cherry shifted his chair a little closer to Denis. "If I'm wrong, no harm."

"He's a friend." Denis shook his head. "But that's neither here nor there. Tell me about the arrest."

"You don't wanna know where I've been before that?" Cherry had to remind himself they'd been a one-time thing. *So far. One time so far.* His brain wasn't helpful in staying on task. "Never mind, but I wanna know all those little things about you soon."

"Let's start with the arrest, see where we go from there."

Chapter Ten

Denis

They had their thirty-minute conference, then Denis opened the door and motioned the bailiff over. "Tell the judge we're ready."

Ten minutes inside the courtroom and the charges were dropped, Cherry released. While the bailiff took him to get his property, Denis took a chance and made a call. "Carole, get a hold of impound's supervisor. Tell them the judge dropped the charges, and Mr. Palant's bike isn't evidence."

"Might be hard to get confirmation to them this late. It's nearly midnight, Denis." Carole's voice didn't hint at fatigue or annoyance, just straight to work. "But I know someone I can use as a runner first thing in the morning. Don't count on getting it out tonight."

"Okay. Thanks." He paused, grinning, "Carole, tell your boss he's not paying you enough to still be at the office this late."

"Who said I was at the office." The line clicked as the call disconnected, and Denis chuckled.

They walked out together, shoulders rubbing. Denis slowed and turned, asking, "What else do you have planned for the night?"

Cherry shrugged. "You said I can't get my bike out of impound until tomorrow." He thumped his phone against his leg before shoving it in his pocket. Denis noted how the leather vest with the club's name across the back rode his shoulders as if tailored to fit. "Phone's dead, so I can't even call for a ride. I've got nothing pressing. You?"

Denis crowded a little closer. "I was just thinking."

"Yeah? About what?" Cherry's grin was playing around the corners of his mouth. "I assume you do lots of lawyerly thinking."

Denis see-sawed one hand, then placed it in the center of Cherry's chest. "I was thinking we could go back to mine. Get some sleep."

Cherry laughed and leaned into Denis' touch. "I could be convinced. If you're really offering, that is."

"Oh, I'm more than offering." Denis pressed closer. "I'm insisting."

***

Cherry

Cherry didn't know what hit harder, the sharp creak of Denis' bedframe under their weight or the way the man's breath hitched when Cherry's hands found his hips. The room was dark, save for the slash of streetlight cutting through the blinds, painting Denis' bare chest in silver and shadow.

They'd stumbled in from the courthouse, shedding clothes like old skin. Cherry had folded his vest with normal reverence before losing his shirt, then pulling at Denis' tie, a trail of fabric marking their path from living room to mattress. The air was thick with the musk of sweat and want, and Cherry's pulse hammered in his throat as Denis sprawled beneath him, eyes dark and daring.

"Condom's in the drawer," Denis murmured, voice rough, one hand sliding down Cherry's chest, nails grazing ink and muscle. "Lube too. You're driving tonight, Cherry."

Cherry's gut clenched, heat pooling low. He'd been here before...well, not *here*, not like this, but the mechanics weren't foreign. Women, sure, back when he was still trying to play the part, but this was different. Denis was all hard planes and stubble, with a body that met his strength with its own, and the thought of sinking into him, of claiming that heat, made Cherry's hands shake as he fumbled for the nightstand. Denis grinned, lazy and wicked, propping up on his elbows to watch.

"Nervous, biker boy?"

"Oh, fuck off," Cherry growled, but there was no bite in it, just a laugh, low and unsteady, as he ripped the foil with his teeth. He slicked himself up, the latex cold against his throbbing cock, then coated his fingers, meeting Denis' gaze. "You sure?"

Denis arched a brow, spreading his thighs wider, one hand tugging Cherry closer by the waistband of his still-open jeans. "Been sure since I saw you dancing in that club. C'mon, gorgeous. Show me what you've got. Don't make me wait."

Cherry leaned in, kissing him hard. There was no finesse to the kiss, all teeth clashing, tongues fighting, all while his fingers slid down, circling, pressing. Denis groaned into his mouth, hips bucking, and Cherry pushed in slow, one finger, then two, feeling the tight heat give way. *Fuck, it was good. Almost too good.* With Denis' gasps, the way his head tipped back, stubble glinting in the half-light, it all conspired to drive Cherry's need higher. He worked him open slowly, each movement deliberate, studying every flicker across Denis' face, every shudder that said he was doing it right.

"Now," Denis panted, gripping Cherry's wrist, guiding him. "Fuck me, Cherry. Now."

Cherry didn't need asking twice. He lined up, one hand braced on Denis' thigh, the other gripping the headboard, and pushed in, slow at first, inch by inch, until Denis' heat swallowed him whole. The sound Denis made was half-growl, half-moan, and it lit Cherry up like a flare, and he rocked deeper, finding a rhythm of in and out. Denis met him thrust for thrust, hands clawing at Cherry's back, nails biting into skin, urging him on. It was messy and raw, a collision of need that drowned out the world. Nothing left but Cherry's grunts, Denis' curses, the slap of flesh, and creak of springs.

"Harder," Denis rasped, locking legs around Cherry's waist, pulling him in tight. Cherry obliged, hips snapping, losing himself in the burn, the stretch, the way Denis' cock leaked against his stomach, untouched and begging. He shifted, angling, and Denis arched, a ragged "Fuck, right there" spilling out as Cherry hit that spot again and again.

It built fast, a savage pressure coiling tight in Cherry's spine, and he reached between them, wrapping a fist around Denis, stroking rough and quick. Denis came first, breathing out on a choked shout, the cum hot and wet across Cherry's hand, and the sight of those dark eyes, pupils blown wide, mouth slack, it all worked to shove Cherry over the edge. He buried himself deep and ground harder, trying to climb inside Denis, groaning low as he spilled, the world blurring into heat and Denis' ragged breathing.

They collapsed together, a tangle of sweat-slick limbs, Cherry's face pressed to Denis' neck, tasting salt and the heat from a ragged pulse. Neither moved, just breathed, the aftershocks humming between them. Denis' hand found Cherry's hair, threading through it, and Cherry let himself sink into it, the weight of the night settling like a brand on his soul.

Denis stirred, and Cherry shivered as a finger trailed across the tattoos on his shoulder. "What's this one for? Why a bulldog?"

Cherry chuckled. "Not every tattoo has a story behind it." He shifted and looked at his shoulder. "Sometimes it's just about having extra money. But this one does have meaning. It's a memorial, see the dates?" He worked the condom off his wilting cock and tied it off, dropping it on the floor at the side of the bed.

Denis angled his head to look at the tattoo closer. "I do now. Is it for friends you've lost?" His hand covered the tattoo, the touch warm and certain.

"No, it's men we lost in Iraq. My group was a forwards echelon, and we took all the chances. The Taliban couldn't beat us, but it was a war of attrition. Every week we'd get a new guy. My role was to try and keep everyone alive." He shrugged. "I couldn't save everyone, but I fucking tried."

Denis leaned closer, lips trailing across Cherry's skin. "If it could have been done, you'd have done it." He kissed the tattoo again, then pulled back slightly. "And your role in the IMC is similar, right? You keep everyone safe?"

"Kinda." Cherry bent to capture Denis' lips. "I do what I can."

"Oh, I think you do just fine." Denis pushed Cherry flat on the mattress and climbed up to straddle his hips. "I think I should verify you do just fine. If you're up for it?"

Cherry arched his neck, asking for kisses without verbalizing the need. Denis bent down, teeth and lips cutting a path down his throat. Cherry strained up, cock already at half-mast. "I'm up for it, Denis. Oh, yeah."

Chapter Eleven

Cherry

Morning light stabbed through the blinds, too bright, too sharp, and Cherry squinted against it, Denis' arm slung heavy across his chest. The bed smelled like them, lots of sex and a little sleep, and for a moment, he let it hold him, the steady rise of Denis' breathing syncing with his own. He turned his head, catching the lawyer's profile. Plush lips were barely parted, dark lashes in stark relief against his skin—seeing him like that made something soft twist in Cherry's gut, a warmth he hadn't earned yet.

He stretched out and grabbed the plug for his phone that had come disconnected. It took a couple of seconds to boot up, then his phone buzzed, a relentless rattle on the floor next to where his jeans lay crumpled. Once, twice, a dozen times, the damn thing wouldn't quit, and reality crashed in like a fist through glass. The club. Diesel. Busk. Ruger. The impound. *Fuck*. He'd ghosted them, his brothers, his family, lost in Denis' sheets while they'd likely been scrambling. Guilt clawed up his throat, bitter and cold, and he eased completely out from under Denis' arm, snatching the phone.

Forty-seven missed calls. Texts stacked like a rap sheet. Busk's all caps *WHERE THE FUCK ARE YOU*, Rook's *Diesel's stable, you good?*, even a prospect's shaky *VP's pissed, man*. Cherry's stomach dropped, thumbs hovering over the screen, no reply big enough to fix it.

"Cherry?" Denis' voice, sleep-rough, cut through the spiral. He propped up on one elbow, hair a mess, eyes narrowing. "You look like someone died. What's up?"

Cherry blew out a breath, tossing the phone onto the bed between them. "Forgot to boot the phone. And the club, man. They've been blowing me up all night. My brother went down, that was the bike wreck. Man, I was supposed to..." He trailed off, jaw tight. "I fucked up."

Denis sat up fully, sheets pooling at his waist, and the concern in his eyes hit Cherry harder than the guilt. "Hey, slow down. They're pissed 'cause they care, right? Tell me about them."

Cherry hesitated, then leaned back against the headboard, staring at the ceiling. "Incoherent MC. My crew. After I left the Marines, after twenty-two years in, you know? I was just done with the military. They had failed not only me, but every one of my brothers in the Corp. That bullshit left me drifting. Circling the drain, you know? Then I met Busk, he's our VP now, way back when he was just a patched grunt. Pulled me in slow, but it stuck. They're my family. Chosen, not blood, but tighter than anything I ever had. Richer for it, every damn day." He glanced at Denis, half-expecting a smirk, but found quiet instead, a nod that said he understood, and Cherry took him at his word.

"Sounds like something worth keeping," Denis said, voice low. "Wish I had that kinda anchor sometimes." He stopped, shaking his head with a rueful grin. "That's a story for date number two. Or three."

Cherry blinked, then laughed, the sound coming out rough, but real. "Date, huh? That what this is?"

Denis leaned in, brushing a kiss along Cherry's jaw, slow and deliberate. "Damn right it is. You in?"

"Yeah," Cherry murmured, turning into it, catching Denis' lips for a soft, lingering press. "I'm in."

Chapter Twelve

Denis

The impound lot was a graveyard of rust and rubber, Cherry's bike gleaming like a beacon among the wrecks. The bike wasn't the only thing that demanded attention. IMC had shown up in force.

Denis took in the line of leather and chrome from across the lot. There was a large contingent of IMC, all standing attentively, the man Cherry had described as the VP at the helm like a goddamn general. He'd expected a representative for the club to show based on what he could hear from his side of Cherry's call earlier. But he wasn't prepared for the sheer presence of the bikers standing quietly, in a formation, even as each man looked like he could swing into action without warning. As they drove past, he could see the VP was a wall of a man, broad and scarred, and the way he stalked towards the gate of the impound yard made Denis' throat tighten.

"How are you explaining me?" That wasn't something he'd heard on his end of Cherry's phone call, and right now? It felt like he'd left it late.

Cherry blew out a hard breath. "If I said I was done hiding that part of me, how would you feel?"

Denis immediately had a rush of adrenaline, tamping it down as if he were doing a difficult and contentious deposition. "If you are doing it for you, that's something I'd be a hundred percent behind." He paused. "But, and this isn't me telling you that I'm not in favor, but if you're doing it for me, then that's the wrong reason." Cherry's immediate chuckle, low and filled with affection, made him smile as he cut his gaze to rest on Cherry's face.

"I'm so tired of playing a part in life. I'd rather write my own story."

Denis waited for Cherry to continue, and when it was clear he was done speaking, asked, "You're not risking your place in the club, are you?"

Cherry's response was immediate, "I hope not, the IMC's former VP is in a throuple relationship, and the other man that's the tripod in that little love tangle is still a rival club's officer, the Caddo Hobos, CoBos. So no, they won't give me shit about you. Maybe shit about hiding something from everyone, but not about you." Cherry's fingers grazed along Denis' throat. "Now if you were a prosecutor, it might be different." When Denis looked back at him, Cherry laughed long and low. "Just fuckin' with you. I expect you'll be welcomed."

Denis pulled his car into the parking on the other side of the little kiosk at the entrance. "Might as well get this over with, I guess." He parked and unbuckled, turning in the seat as he shut off the car. Over Cherry's shoulder he could see the line of men was bending in the middle, the tall man taking point as they all stalked their direction.

Cherry slid out of the passenger seat, all easy swagger, but Denis caught the flicker in his eyes. It was nerves, maybe, or anticipation.

Chapter Thirteen

Cherry

Cherry smirked and winked at Denis before stepping forwards as Busk closed in, the VP's boots kicking up dust. The big man squinted, then grinned. Cherry gripped Busk's arm in a warrior's clasp, their heads knocking together, Busk's fist pounding Cherry's back like he was hammering steel.

"Well, shit, brother. It's about time you brought around someone worth a damn. You fucking asshole motherfucker. Ruger's gonna fuckin' love this." Busk's fist pounded Cherry's back again, harder. "We thought you'd been disappeared by the po-lice. Nobody could find you in the jail, and nobody had a lead on where you might be. Fuck, brother." Another pounding against his back. "Fuck, man."

Cherry's laugh was muffled against Busk's shoulder. "Can't say I'm sorry, brother. Night of my life."

The gate clattered open and a man appeared, rolling Cherry's motorcycle over the gravel. "I need to pay the impound." He pulled back.

Busk shook his head. "Man told me there wasn't a fee. Your guy worked some magic and the goddammed bogus charges were dropped, too. Better news, that rookie is gonna get a good old talking to. That fuckin' cop was so green he needed a keeper."

***

Denis

Denis hung back, watching Cherry greet the members, then begin what looked like a complex greeting ritual with the bike, going over nearly every inch with soft hands.

Busk was on him in a moment, a freight train in leather, pulling Denis into his own one-armed hug that damn near cracked his spine. "Cherry's Guy," Busk rumbled, stepping back to size him up. "Good to meet'cha. My boy did alright for himself. I'm Busk, VP of the Baton Rouge chapter of the motherfuckin' IMC. We've got a big meeting tomorrow with all the chapter heads, as well as all the crew from Mother. That shit's club only, so you'll have to give him up for a while. There's room for family on day two, we'll do a big cookout for everyone. Expect to see you there, hear me?" All Denis could do was nod. "Good talk." Busk turned on his heel, striding back to where Cherry stood next to his bike. "Say your goodbyes to your guy, brother. We're rolling. Places to be."

Cherry's grin hit Denis in the center of his chest, wide and bright. Cherry fired up the bike, the growl vibrating through Denis, then swaggered over, grabbing Denis' hand. "My Guy," he said, voice low, tugging him close. "Kinda like the sound of that."

"Me too," Denis murmured, brushing a kiss across Cherry's lips, heat flaring at the contact. "So that's Busk, huh? Text me later. We'll sort that next date."

Cherry grinned, stole another quick kiss, then swung onto his bike. The IMC roared out in a double line, Cherry beside Busk, and Denis watched them into the distance, the impound gate clanging shut behind him.

Chapter Fourteen
Cherry

The clubhouse was a hive when they rolled in, prospects scurrying like ants under Busk's rapid-fire barked orders. Cherry parked his bike in its usual spot, the engine's heat still ticking as he swung off, boots hitting dirt. He braced for the third degree of questions about where he'd been, who he'd been with, but Busk went straight to business, clapping him on the shoulder. "Meeting's tomorrow. We're gonna need a good solution for the fucking MC pushing our lines. The goddamned Azrael's Scimitars, outta Lafayette. Gonna need the clubhouse space locked down."

Cherry nodded, falling into step, the shift to work mode snapping him straight. "Prospects on perimeter until and during the meeting?"

"Until, during, after, you use your best judgement on prospects and probationary patches, but hangarounds are out. Our clubhouse is members only 'til this shit's settled. Let's take it a step further and say only brothers in good standing are allowed in for the meeting. I don't think we've got any deadbeat members, but this'll be a good test of that." Busk jerked his chin at a skinny kid hauling beer crates. "Yo, man. Get those inside, now. Shit should have already been handled."

Cherry took over, voice cutting through the chaos. He pointed at several men in succession. "You. Finish setting up chairs for fifty, no, let's say sixty chairs. You. Make sure the ice is stocked, and the bar is ready. Move." The prospects jumped to work, giving Cherry time to organize the hangarounds to be cleared out within a couple of hours, and he felt the rhythm settle into him, the club's heartbeat, steady under his skin. He spent time with each prospect, ensuring they understood their role during the meeting, and then just as importantly, during the family party, where all members and families would be present.

Busk picked that moment to shout across the yard, "Don't forget to bring your Guy, Cherry!" and the entire crew hooted, a prospect snickering until Cherry's glare shut him down cold. His face burned, but he raised a hand, owning it. Denis wasn't a secret. And neither was he. Not anymore, not here, not with them.

He ducked inside, checking the meeting room where the main table was polished best as it could be with all the scars scattered across the surface. He verified the bylaws were pinned to the wall, ashtrays lined up on the table like soldiers. The Azrael's Scimitars were a thorn, encroaching on IMC turf along the I-10 corridor, and tomorrow's sit-down with the IMC chapter heads would set the tone. Push back or bleed out. Cherry's fists flexed, the enforcer in him itching to swing, but he reined it in. Words first. *Always*.

***

Denis

Denis sprawled on his couch that night, beer in hand, the TV droning some cop show he wasn't watching. His phone buzzed, Cherry's name lighting the screen, and he grinned, thumbing it open. *Talk soon* had turned into *Meeting's tomorrow, shit heating up. You good for the cookout day after?*

He typed back, *Wouldn't miss it. Stay safe, biker boy.*

The reply was quick: *Always. Night, lawyer man.*

Denis set the phone down, staring at the ceiling. The IMC was Cherry's world. It was rough and loud, a family forged in steel and loyalty, and Denis would be stepping into it mostly blind. He'd defended bikers before, knew the code, the stakes, but this was personal now. *Cherry's Guy.* Busk's welcome had been a shock, warm and bruising, and Denis surprised himself with how much he wanted in and wanted to see Cherry in his element, wanted to belong somewhere that fierce.

Sleep came slow, Cherry's voice in his head, that low growl promising more.

***

Cherry

The meeting room was a pressure cooker the next day, air thick with smoke and tension. Chapter presidents lined the table with Hammond's Prez, a grizzled bastard named Wildman, at the head, with their own Prez Ruger sitting beside, and Busk at Ruger's right, Cherry standing behind like a sentinel. The Azrael's Scimitars had balls, pushing weed runs into IMC territory, and Wildman laid it out cold: "They hit our edges again, we hit back. Hard."

Cherry nodded, arms crossed, his mind half on Denis, safe back in his lawyer world, and half on the fight brewing. "Got a crew ready," he said, voice steady. "Baton Rouge can hold the line."

Wildman grunted approval, and Busk clapped Cherry's shoulder. "Good. Keep 'em tight." The plan slowly solidified, with talk and planning continuing on for hours. Cherry agreed that the patrols would be doubled, and they'd planned a message to the Scimitars via a torched stash house the other club had claimed. No blood was on the menu yet, but the threat hung heavy.

When it broke, Cherry stepped outside, the night cool against his skin. He texted Denis, *Meeting's done. Cookout's on. You in?*

The reply was instant, *Hell yeah. See you tomorrow.*

***

Cherry

Standing next to his idling bike, Cherry watched as the members tapped for the run pushed through the thick layer of bushes next to the crumbling house. They'd already verified it was uninhabited, enough untracked dirt in the road it was clear nobody had been to it since at least the last rain. He saw the first member through a window, then the bloom of flame behind him.

"Looking good," Busk said, standing next to Cherry.

"Long as they don't have any explosives in there, this looks real good." He grinned. "Confident Pony would have had the receipts if there were any boom boom in the room."

"Smart man who trusts Pony." Busk agreed.

The members returned, every ass was on a bike before Cherry gave the order to roll out. He and Busk were playing tailgunner for the home part of the run, knowing if there was any danger to the column, it would come from the back. Nothing happened, in fact the run home was so textbook it was nearly boring.

Wildman met them at the door, giving every member a rough greeting, telling them without words that Mother appreciated their good works of the night.

Tomorrow was the cookout.

Cherry smiled.

Chapter Fifteen

Denis

The cookout attendees were sprawled across the clubhouse yard, a chaos of leather, kids, and chatter. There were half a dozen grills roaring, nearly a hundred bikes gleaming, and vests with IMC colors everywhere. Denis pulled up, nerves jangling, and quickly spotted Cherry by a picnic table, beer in hand, laughing with a woman who had Busk's eyes. His sister, maybe? Cherry saw him and the change in expression was instant, a grin splitting his face wide as he waved Denis over.

"Denis," Cherry said, tugging him close, arm sliding around his waist. "Meet the family."

It was a whirlwind with Busk pounding his back again, Wildman nodding approval, an introduction to the man who was effectively Cherry's boss, Baton Rouge's president, Ruger. He'd been presented to a dozen patched brothers, them and their old ladies shaking his hand. Cherry stayed glued to his side, possessive and proud, and Denis felt it. That thing he'd hoped for in the warm, unreserved welcome, the sense of belonging, it distinctly felt like a puzzle piece clicking into place.

There was a tense interaction with a prospective member, who Denis now knew could be identified via their vest. The man had shoulder-checked Denis, rocking him back on his heels. Only Cherry's arm around his shoulders kept him from taking a tumble.

"The fuck you think you're doing?" Cherry's clipped words struck the prospect like a lash. Before he'd finished talking, he'd moved and put Denis behind him, effectively protecting him against one of his own. Denis sucked in a harsh breath. This was not how his introduction to the club members who were Cherry's family was supposed to go. *Does it matter the standing in the club? Of course it matters. How can I best help Cherry. By staying silent, I think. Okay, be quiet. Hey Denis, all this is in your brain.* He had to fight against laughter, the tension in the moment stripping away any sense of humor.

The prospect straightened his spine, chin in the air just asking for a punch to pound it down. "He's a fuckin' queer. And a lawyer? You should have your patches cut, my man." The prospect's words dropped into the space around them, silence rolling out from the center of the conflict.

"Cherry, it's okay." Denis had heard much worse through the years. *Ah god. How can I help?* This was rapidly turning into the worst possible outcome.

"The fuck it is."

The muscles in Cherry's shoulders flexed, hands swinging freely at his sides as he took the two swift strides putting him directly in the man's face. The stress of the moment pushed at the bubble of happiness Denis had been walking through. He reached out and grabbed the waistband of Cherry's jeans, needing that anchor to get him through the moment. *It's all going sideways.*

"Prospect, you wanna repeat what you said?" Cherry was staring the man down. "I'd like to know I got it right."

"No." The word was a clipped bludgeon, falling from the prospect's mouth. His face was turning a bright red, and he'd taken a couple of steps backwards and away from Cherry, that defiant chin falling to his chest. "I got it wrong, Enforcer."

Cherry followed him, staying in the man's face. Denis followed, his grip dragging him the small distance. "Yeah, you fucking did. You got it all shades of wrong. Busk, you hear that bullshit this prospect spewed?" Busk stepped up next to Cherry, both men essentially shielding Denis from the unhappy man.

"I did. Sounds like a fucktard to me. Our brother Rook sponsored him, what do you want done to make sure he understands the errors of his ways?"

"Bastard mentioned cutting my patches. I think losing his prospect patch should be good. Bust him back to hangaround status."

"Makes sense to me," Busk drawled. "Rook, come get your prospect, brother."

Cherry turned around, gaze flicking across Denis' face. "You good?" There was a scuffle with the prospect who was pleading his case to a circle of stone-faced men. Cherry ignored the activity at his back. "Denis." Cherry reached out and put an arm around Denis' shoulders. "Are you good?"

"Yeah. I've heard much worse. It just surprised me."

Cherry chuckled, the sound seeming to trail fingers across Denis' skin. "He's made his first mistake. We generally give them two fuckups before we kick them. Cutting him was the right thing to do."

"Cutting him?" Denis had a sudden vision of the man bleeding.

"His prospect patch, yeah. Not the asshole himself."

"Makes more sense." Denis moved to stand next to Cherry, making sure to keep Cherry's arm wrapped around his shoulders. "So, wanna walk around for a bit? You can introduce me as your Guy if you want."

"I want." Cherry laughed softly, huffs of his breath brushing along Denis' throat. "I definitely want." Cherry led him across the expanse of grass behind the clubhouse. "Let's get you introduced."

"Surprised me," Cherry murmured later, lips brushing Denis' ear as they leaned against his bike, the party humming around them. "They're my family, and they took you in like you're theirs too."

Denis grinned, stealing a kiss, tasting beer and Cherry. "Guess I'm Cherry's Guy for real."

"Yeah, you are," Cherry growled, pulling him tighter. "And I'm keeping you."

Chapter Sixteen

Denis

The phone at his elbow rang, dragging Denis' attention off a brief he'd been reading for one of his junior associates. He picked it up, expecting Carole, but got Ricky instead. After brief pleasantries, very brief, Ricky gave him a readout off the Marcus Warner investigation.

"Kid's a short runner. Caine, the supplier, doesn't give Warner a lot of leash to deal. That's one of the reasons he got picked up, someone had called in about a suspicious youth who'd been at a known dealer's house multiple times over a weekend." Ricky's voice deepened. "He's a scared kid, but he might have reason to be. I think in addition to being a short runner for motherfucking Caine, he's being an informer to his cousin. That would be his second cousin twice removed on his momma's side, name of Herbert LaBlanc. That cousin being the same asshole that tried to book your IMC guy."

Denis let the silence grow between them for a moment, then took a deep breath and blew it out. "I find it interesting that he's tied in with that guy." He and Ricky were both on the same page about the rookie, especially since Ricky had taken it upon himself to check into the man. What they'd found was the asshole was rapidly making a name for himself with drug arrests. "You think he's feeding LaBlanc details?"

"Enough to get him to the right place at the right time for probable cause. He claims the arrest, touts it as instinct or a hunch, and looks good to the brass." Ricky made a grumpy sound. "Those arrests doubled after Marcus Warner was picked up. That's a suspicious coincidence to me."

"When you say Marcus is a short runner, how short?" That role was typically given to the least trusted member of a dealer's crew. Couple of hundred dollars of dope, single transaction. "Is he doubled on yet?" Being doubled would mean Marcus was right on the edge of being eliminated. Having to send two runners for a short run was not an efficient use of the dealer's crew.

"No, not doubled up, not yet. If another customer falls to the asshole LaBlanc though, it might be enough suspicion to bring Warner down without even further management." Ricky grunted. "He's just a kid, Denis. I doubt he understands the danger he's in. We need someone to talk to him who isn't a PI or a lawyer."

"You're thinking Cherry? I don't want to involve him if we can help it. Especially with LaBlanc being Marcus's cousin."

"I think we're at the place where there aren't any other real options, Denis." Silence hung between them for a moment, then Ricky said, "Give it a think. Let me know. I'll stick to the kid for now."

"Like glue."

The line went dead and Denis lightly rubbed circles on his temples. After a couple minutes he picked up his cell phone and sent Cherry a text, *Might need your help on a case. No pressure. Let's discuss soon?*

A few minutes later he got a response, *Be at your place by 8 2nite*

The shorthand text made him grin. He knew it killed Cherry to be less than a hundred percent correct in his communications, so he had to be on the road.

"One more endearing trait for my guy."

"When do I get to meet this man who is so endearing?"

Denis looked at the woman in the doorway. "Mother, I didn't hear Carole announce you."

Carole appeared over his mother's shoulder. "I didn't. She beat me to the door."

His mother turned around, hard eyes narrowing as she stared at Carole. "I don't need announcing." She tipped her head to the side. "What do you know about Denis' endearing guy?"

Carole lifted her chin. "More than you do, apparently."

"Ladies, please. Don't fight. Not today. Leave that for the family reunion."

Carole shook her head but his mother turned to look at him. "We don't fight."

"You literally were just fighting." He rose from his desk chair and crossed the width of the room. "Hello, Mother."

Carole snorted, "Mother. That's a riot. I've mothered you more than Carlotta here."

"Just because you're my twin doesn't mean I want to share my child with you." His mother scowled, the expression enhancing the wrinkles on her face telling everyone that was a standard look. "Get your own. Denis is mine."

"Denis is mine, actually." Cherry's voice came from just outside the room.

His mother and Carole whirled around so fast, Denis started laughing.

"Cherry, I'd like to introduce my mother Carlotta, and her twin who is also the heart of my practice, my Aunt Carole. Ladies." Denis pushed past them and into the hallway. He pulled Cherry in for a quick kiss, then turned to look at the two women, both with their mouths open. "This is my Guy."

***

Cherry

He nearly laughed, but held in the amusement because both women looked like someone to take offense easily. He didn't want his introduction to them to go sideways because they both looked like a cat had pissed in their favorite pair of shoes.

He took the more peaceful route, with a "Ladies, good to meet you." His arm went around Denis' waist, and he gave a squeeze, receiving one in return. "Denis, I believe we had some business to deal with?" Lifting one eyebrow, he looked up at Denis, waiting for a cue of how things were going to go.

Denis swooped down and stole another quick kiss. "Yes, we have so much business to deal with." He didn't quite grind on Cherry's leg, but it was a close movement. "So much."

"Carlotta, why don't you and I go have a cup of coffee. You can catch me up on the family news." Carole turned the woman and bustled them both up the hallway to the elevator. Cherry lost sight of them when Denis pulled him backwards into his office.

"I didn't know Carole was your aunt." He lifted his chin in a clear demand that Denis met with a slower, deeper kiss. "I don't want to talk about your female relatives right now, though." Another kiss, this more demanding, Denis' tongue lashing across the seam of Cherry's lips and he opened invitingly.

This kiss stole all thoughts as Cherry followed Denis' lead. They wound up sprawled across a loveseat, Denis pulling Cherry down on top of him. Now there was most definitely a crotch grinding on his leg, and he groaned.

"Gonna make me come just like this."

Arms locked around Cherry's neck, holding him in place. The kiss deepened again, growing more erotic as Denis alternated teeth and tongue to steal Cherry's sensibility.

"Denis, I'm gonna come."

"Me too, baby. Me too."

"The door is still open." He broke the kiss and looked over his shoulder to see the door slowly closing. Carole and Carlotta both were peering around the edge of the door. "Goddamn, Denis."

When the door finally settled into its frame, Denis rolled them towards the back of the little sofa until they were face-to-face.

"That's my mom. She's a piece of work. Carole was a savior for me, both a safe place and an understanding adult to help me through the realization that girls would never do it for me. Carole's in the only family picture I own, in my home." His hands cupped around Cherry's jaw, pulling him closer. "And I don't want to talk about them again, not now, and not ever when we're being intimate." His nose wrinkled like he smelled something foul. "No, just no."

Cherry pushed forwards, gaining a little leverage so he could hover over Denis, even if it was at a slant. "I don't want to talk about anything except my cock in your ass. And I wasn't thinking of it, not really, but I did bring a condom and some lube. To our business discussion."

"Pretty sure of yourself, aren't you?" Denis grinned and angled his head for another kiss. "Cock in ass sounds like a solid plan. I'm happy to be the bottom today."

"Before or after our business meeting. If there actually was one?" He arched an eyebrow.

"Was the text a ruse? I'm fine with it either way, but just checking."

"Gah." Denis ground hard against Cherry's thigh. "We should do business first." He pulled his hips back in small increments. "Goddamn it to hell." He lunged in for a hard kiss. "I fucking hate you."

"And I hate you," he responded, grinning.

Chapter Seventeen

Denis

He pulled in a few hard breaths and rolled away from Cherry. But he misjudged the distance and rolled himself flat on the floor. He was staring up when Cherry's face came into view.

"Babe, you okay?"

The bastard had the bad taste to grin.

By the time Denis had shoved his way to a sitting position, Cherry was up and standing with one hand out. Denis considered not taking the help for about half a second, then he reached for the assistance. A moment later, he was on his feet.

"That's annoying."

"What, babe?" This was Cherry, doing his best to hide a smile.

"And that's extra annoying. First you push me off the couch, then you yank me up in like an instant, and now you're laughing at me." He straightened his collar. "Business meeting protocol means not throwing me on the floor, no matter the injuries I might acquire."

"Protocol." Cherry took a step forwards. "Acquire." He took another step. "You're extra hot when you go all lawyerly." The next step had them chest-to-chest. "Extra hot."

Denis wrapped his arms around Cherry and pulled him closer. "What are you talking about?"

Cherry initiated the kiss, stretching up to press their lips together. "I'm talking about how hot you are when you pull out the lawyer side of you. I foresee some roleplay in our future."

"The motion to allow roleplay of lawyer and client or any other option of said roleplay is hereby approved by said lawyer." He chuckled and gave Cherry another squeeze. "Commencement of said roleplay is to be at initiation by either party to this agreement. But not before today's business meeting is concluded to everyone's satisfaction." Cherry chased his mouth for another kiss.

"Commencement of said business meeting to begin in five, four—" another kiss interrupted the countdown "—two, one."

Cherry stole another kiss before stepping back.

"Was that really your mother?"

"Oh, yeah. That was Carlotta at her...well, not finest, because she can get on a roll and stay there. But yes, that was my mother. And Carole is my aunt, her twin sister. Who I get on with so much better than Mother." He pulled in a breath and turned to face the windows. "Give me two minutes to get my libido under control."

Breath ghosted across the back of his neck as Cherry chuckled. "Libido is a more interesting word than a pending motion."

Denis tipped his chin up, staring at the ceiling. "Zeus give me strength."

"Zeus? The god Zeus? Is there something you wanna tell me about your daddy?" Hands gripped his traps, fingers and thumb working deep into the tense muscles. "Because that's not a meeting I think should be left up to chance."

"No, my dad was not a god. Not even close to it. He's the reason I went into law to begin with, because he was a politician. Was, not is, because he didn't stick with that any longer than he did the role of dad." Denis let his head hang loose, enjoying the impromptu neck rub. "He's somewhere in Taiwan, last I heard news. Doubt he knows I still exist, much less that I'm now back in Baton Rouge. Coast is clear as far as I'm concerned." Breathing slowly, he deliberately relaxed the muscles Cherry was working over. "Your folks still around?" The fingers on his neck paused for a couple of beats, then resumed.

"Nope, they died in a car accident while I was deployed. Buried and memorialized long before I learned of the accident. Only one sibling, a brother. He went in the Marines about eight years behind me. Still in as far as I know. And that's my unclose family in a nutshell." Cherry gave his neck a final squeeze and stepped back.

The skin of Denis' neck felt chilled, and he wondered if he'd turned over the wrong rock with his question. *Gotta believe he'll tell me if I did.* "So, the business end of this. Wanna sit and have a conversation?"

"Here as opposed to me finally getting you on the back of my bike?" Cherry grinned and winked at him. The opportunity hadn't yet come around that they were both ready to be vertical instead of horizontal, and on the road instead of behind closed doors.

"Here, I guess. I have a couple of favors to ask, and I want your honest response to them both."

***

Cherry

"Lay it on me. Can't advise if I don't know the topic." Cherry looked around and pointed to an upholstered chair near the couch. "Mind if I sit there? I've been on the road since about this time last night."

"Yes, please. Sit. Want a bottle of water?" Denis walked behind the desk and opened the door of a mini-fridge. "I'm getting one."

"Sure." He shook his head. "How do you switch gears so fast? Ten minutes ago we were both about to come in our pants, and now we're making small talk?"

Denis grinned as he tossed the bottle to Cherry. "Compartmentalization, my guy. I'm still half-chubbed up." He pulled the second chair closer to where Cherry sat. "So the business part." Denis blew out a stream of air. "Before we met, I started a case pro bono for a small-time drug runner. His grandmother was adamant he wasn't in as much trouble as the charges indicated. I put one of my PIs on him, and sure enough, nothing is as it seems. He's a runner for a larger player, Caine—"

"I know of Caine. He's a real asshole." Cherry grimaced. "Sorry, it was just a name I knew. Carry on."

Denis shook his head. "No worries, it's not a timed presentation, just me talking through what I know. So, back to what I know is that Caine isn't trusting this kid anymore. He's only sending him out on less lucrative runs, and he's got a babysitter. Kid is named Marcus Warner, and we, me and my PI, think he's turned confidential informant to his cousin. Said cousin is a rookie in the BRPD who's building a name for himself on successful drug arrests."

"Okay." Cherry shook his head. "Not sure where I come in. I expect you could get your pro bono client off lightly if there's police corruption for the press to focus on. Where do I come in?"

"I'd like you to talk to this kid, Marcus Warner, about his cousin. But that cousin is sort of attached to you. Kind of. In a way I don't want to bring up." Denis screwed up his face again, this time as if smelling something rancid.

BRPD, rookie, kind of attached to me. Cherry met Denis' gaze head on. "LaBlanc, right? That's the cousin?" Denis gave a short nod. "So I talk to this Marcus Warner, verify what you think is going on, and then what? Am I supposed to give the kid protection or something? Would you expect me to go testify in court? Wouldn't our relationship come up, along with the dismissed charges brought by the LaBlanc asshole? What am I supposed to do here, Denis?"

"That's what I hoped we could talk about. Ricky, my PI, doesn't think Warner would talk to either of us. We don't know if he's got a connection with the club, but if a random biker appeared in a bar on a stool next to him, that biker could give some wisdom about Caine. I know there's a ton of suppositions in that statement alone, but there's something about this kid. It hit me, and it hit Ricky. Warner could be something, anything other than a short, doubled runner for a scumbag like Caine."

"Okay. Gotcha, gotcha." Cherry ran a couple of possible proposals through his head. "Does he need a full change of range? Like leaving the 'hood? Does he have any interest in motorcycles or clubs?"

"That would be the best option. Get him right out of the zone." He grabbed his phone off the desk and dialed a preassigned number.

Need to get him to tell me what my number is. Bet it's sixty-nine. He gave himself a mental shake. *Focus, man.*

"Ricky."

A deep voice answered, "Boss?"

"To your knowledge does Warner have any interest in motorcycle clubs or bikes in general?"

There was a pause, then that deep voice said, "Pleased to meet you, Cherry."

Both Denis and Cherry laughed.

"And you, Ricky the famous PI."

"Not as famous as you, Mr. Enforcer of the Baton Rouge IMC. You're pretty damn famous in certain circles."

"I try to keep my business under wraps as much as I can. Must be slacking. I'll get right on that."

Ricky laughed this time. "Maybe I'm just that good."

Denis broke in and when Cherry looked at him the man seemed half pissed. "Back on track, gentlemen. Does Warner have an interest in MCs?"

"Actually, yeah. He does. He's been hanging around the Zebra Tail with some RC guys."

"I know that bar. For IMC it's a halfway point between just being a rider and exploring being a member. We've picked up quite a few hangarounds from there. That's interesting." He looked at Denis. "Do you have a pic of the kid? I can tell you pretty quickly if he's already one of our potentials."

"Yeah, let me just"—Denis picked up the phone—"send you the details."

A moment later, Cherry's phone rang out the top line from an 80s love anthem. "Fuck." He silenced it as quickly as possible but not before both Ricky and Denis were cackling like little old women. "Shut up. I've heard my ringtone on your phone, and it's not something that should be shared publicly."

"Okay, okay." Denis was still laughing as Cherry pulled up the image.

"Yeah, this is Marcus Warner, right? The name didn't hit me until now. We've had him on a couple of charity runs. He's not a hangaround, not yet, but wouldn't take much to bump him up. But if we need him to be disappeared, I'm planning to work on a prospect group in a few days. I'd have to clear it with my bosses, but we could maybe wrap him up in that. We keep a couple of trailers out at the clubhouse for prospects to stay at while going through the wringer. That's what they call my section of education. Cherry's wringer."

***

He looked over the group of men standing in a half-circle around him. Out of eight men, he expected to take two to membership level over the next week. Five would stay prospects for another three months, which would be the end of their ability to stay at that level. They'd either advance or fail out. One man, kid really, would be going to membership status from barely hangaround status.

And hadn't that been a shit conversation with Ruger and Busk?

He was lucky he'd tapped the men on a good night, or they wouldn't have been open to even discussing his plan.

"Busk, got a minute?" His VP turned around and Cherry saw Ruger directly behind him. That sealed it, having both available was a rare occurrence these days. Cherry made a mental note to ask Busk about that little tidbit. "Ruger, it's good you're here. Saves me hunting you down."

"Like you could hunt me." The man stepped around Busk, and Cherry noticed how Busk's hand slipped along Ruger's hip. Well that's an interesting development. "What's up, Enforcer?" That was Ruger's way of determining if this was club business or something personal.

"Prez," he confirmed Ruger's question. "And VP, can we talk privately about a request I

have for you two? Might have to bring in Twisted to yay or nay me." That should tell them how delicate his request was. "Figure if we have to go that high, I better have full support."

"Back room," Busk said with a jerk of his head. "It's empty right now."

Cherry closed the door behind him and started moving to his normal position, standing behind the president's chair. Busk laughed and grabbed his arm, turning him towards a regular officer's chair. "The better to see you, my dear. Don't make the old man crane his neck around to have a chat."

"Yeah. Habits die hard." Cherry sat and forced his breathing to slow. He wanted this, more than he'd thought. Denis thought it was a great idea, and he'd asked. I just wanna..."Up front, this is something my Guy is involved in. You say no, and it's no, and he gets that message. I wanted to put that out there first."

"Appreciate it," Ruger said, sliding back in his seat. His elbows hit the table with a gentle thud. "I liked Chapin. Seems a good fit for you. Glad you got him." He cut his eyes at Busk so quickly Cherry nearly missed it. "Hard to find

someone who understands the life. Good for you."

"So what's the ask?" Busk leaned back, arm slung over the back of the chair next to him, the one Ruger was seated in. And that's not a question I'm gonna ask. "Get it out quick, like pulling a knife."

Ruger laughed. "I think that's yanking off a Band-Aid, not pulling a knife."

"My dude, my president, my friend, we are badassed bikers, we don't fucking mess with Band-Aids."

Cherry chuckled at the banter, which helped relieve his nerves, something he thought they had aimed for. "My Guy has a pro bono case involving a kid who's been on a couple of rides with us. I recognized his picture." He pulled his phone out and navigated to the image, then slid the phone to the two men. "Marcus Warner. Seems a good kid, someone we'd want. But he's tied up with Caine, and has been tied to LaBlanc, too. Distant cousins, and seems like the cop is blackmailing him. Looks like Warner feeds LaBlanc names, places, and times, making the rookie look good."

"Snitch? And you think he's a fit?" Busk blew out a thin stream of air. "Really?" He paused and looked at Cherry. "Did you hit your head recently? That might be the cause of the delusion."

"He's a blackmailed kid who's scared to death. I haven't talked to him yet, but I stopped by Zebra Tail yesterday and he was pale and jumpy as shit. LaBlanc strolled in, dressed in civies, clipped Warner in the ear and led him outside. That's not a willing snitch who's benefiting from his actions. That's someone under threat to perform a particular trick." Cherry slowed his breathing again. "I feel strongly about bringing this kid into the fold, sooner rather than later."

"You don't think this cousin knows the kid's been riding with us? Came out to Zebra Tail to corral him and you don't think the cousin knows? We'd be the first place he'd come looking if Warner fell off the grid." Ruger's head swung back and forth. "How you gonna fix that first stumbling block?"

"You don't think the snitch part is the first block? It is for me. Once a snitch, always a snitch." Busk shook his head.

Ruger cleared his throat and Busk's head snapped his direction. "Not always. Cherry's right that the motive for being an informant holds all the cards. He's not benefiting, other than avoiding whatever kinda hell LaBlanc has promised. I think we'd have to know that first thing before we can really dial in what we're in favor of or against. How can you find that out?"

"Go back to the Zebra Tail and talk to Charli. She knows everything about everything and everyone. If I don't want to ask Warner, and I do not, not until I know if I can offer him sanctuary, Charli is the first up." Both men were nodding by the time he finished. "She on the payroll, so she's a safe bet."

"Sounds like a plan. Find out what kind of black banner LaBlanc has, and we'll see if we can sort it and Warner without bringing additional scrutiny to the club. Since the charges against you were dropped, LaBlanc has stopped and harassed four local members. He's playing it fairly smart, only tapping solo riders. We're going to recommend everyone have a second going forwards." Ruger looked at Busk. "You know, I think I'd like to go to the Zebra tonight." He glanced at Cherry. "I'll be your second."

Busk opened his mouth and then snapped it shut. "Your decision." He pushed away from the table and stalked to the door, leaving without saying anything else.

"Everything okay with him?" Cherry asked and Ruger answered with a wave.

"Let's roll," he said instead. "Can't get there if we never leave."

As they walked through the door of the bar, a fight was just breaking out. Cherry caught the first thrown chair before it could hit Ruger, and then looked to the altercation. Only half surprised it was between Warner and LaBlanc, he turned to Ruger. "Our hand might be forced."

"Then it's forced." Ruger cracked his knuckles. "Let's see what's going on, brother."

Charli was standing on the bar, shouting at the fight, and turned to them and said, "God am I glad to see you. Can you stop this madness?"

Given the perfect opening, Cherry strolled in and caught LaBlanc in a pincher hold from the back, effectively trapping both arms. Warner bent over, arms clutching his midsection.

"He's a fucking queer," LaBlanc shouted. "Not worth anyone's time. His folks aren't going to be so thrilled with their boy now, are they, cuz?"

Meanwhile Ruger stepped in front of Warner and just shook his head, the expression on his face black with rage. Cherry tipped his head to the side as LaBlanc struggled to free himself. Putting his mouth close to LaBlanc's ear, he asked, loud enough the entire bar could hear, "Did you just fucking out someone without their permission?"

"He's just a fucking queer." LaBlanc stared at Warner over Ruger's shoulder.

"Shut your mouth," Ruger said without turning around. "Heard about enough outta you."

Cherry looked around, unsurprised that the bar had emptied with the exception of IMC-tied folks. He adjusted his hold on the man, pulled his pistol, and snapped it hard against the back of LaBlanc's head. Cherry held his weight for a moment before letting him fall to the floor like a puppet whose strings had just been cut. "He's quiet now, boss."

Ruger turned and took in the scene, the darkness fading from his features. "Good call, Enforcer." He turned back to Warner. "Marcus, right?" As expected, having the local president of a club he'd been trying to get into know him snapped up Warner's head, fast. His features were white, mouth pursed in pain, something Cherry recognized.

He grabbed a chair and slipped it behind Warner, using a hand on his shoulder to guide him down. "Cop a squat, dude."

Ruger stepped to Cherry's side. "You've got just a couple of minutes to explain what was going on before LaBlanc is cogent enough to remember anything. Tell me, Marcus, what's going on?"

Warner let his head swing low, shoulders hunched up like wings. "He's family. I can't speak on him."

"Minute and a half left before Cherry and I walk. Talk." Ruger got down on one knee, grunting as he landed. "Fucking shit. Cherry, gonna need a hand up and we're never speaking of this."

Cherry laughed, and felt the muscles of Warner's neck loosen. "Yes, boss," he responded, gave Warner a squeeze and stepped back.

"He's family."

"You already claimed him. Don't know why, but you did. You've been on runs with us, you know what the IMC stands for. We're found family, not just blood, and I like to think our bonds are stronger as a result. What was the fight about just now?"

"He caught me at a club downtown last night. I thought I'd gotten out before he saw me, but no such luck." Warner's head came up, his expression furious. "It shouldn't make anyone no nevermind if I'm a cocksucker. And I am one, you should know that before you say anything else. I can make myself scarce if that's a problem."

"Not a problem for me." Ruger looked up at Cherry. "Problem for you, Enforcer?"

"No, Prez. No problem here." He paused for a moment, deciding, then thought of Denis' face and said, "I'm a cocksucker, too, in case that changes your mind, Marcus." Cherry felt faint for a moment, the enormousness of what he'd just done slamming into him like a freight train.

Warner stared at Cherry for long enough it was uncomfortable. "I saw you, you know? I'd have never said a word, not to you, not to anyone. You dancing with that lawyer, the one working on my arrest, was hella hot."

And now it was Cherry's face that was hot, thinking about that first night he'd met Denis. I should take him out, wine and dine him. He's worth keeping outing myself for. *"Well, that was the first and only time I hit up that club. I appreciate you holding my confidence, even, maybe especially because I didn't know you were."*

"I'm thinking we need to take this elsewhere, or we need to clonk LaBlanc again."

"I don't have my ride. I drove out tonight." Warner hung his head again. "Not something a real biker would do, I know."

"Fuck real, if it's cold I drive my four-wheeler."

"Same here. The grocery getter gets a lotta winter use." Cherry laughed and turned around, watching LaBlanc trying to wrangle being enough upright to take a sitting position. He stepped closer and swept his foot under the

propping arm, dropping LaBlanc back to the ground with a thud. "He's out again, but I'm with Prez. We need to vacate. Marcus, we'll have you follow us, if you can drive?"

"He only got one hit in before you guys stopped him." Warner pushed to his feet. "I'm in your debt no matter what."

"Tell Denis that I was the good guy, payment enough." Cherry grinned. "Let's roll."

Which brought him to this first round of training with the men wanting to wear an IMC patch.

"How many of you prefer to talk your way out of a fight?"

Five men lifted a hand, glancing around the half-circle.

"Okay." He pointed to each man who hadn't taken the easy answer, "You, you, and you, don't let the door hit'cha where the good Lord split'cha." He made a shooing motion. "Go on, git. This isn't for you."

One of the men reared up, pushing his chest out as his cheeks got tomato-red. "You can't cut me. This is my third chance."

"Which means it is your last chance. You didn't even make it to the Enforcer talk the other two times. If you want to petition for additional time, talk to Twisted." He watched the blood drain from the man's face. "I'm sure he'd be happy to hear why you got booted."

"Least Twisted has some balls. Talk my way out of a fight? Who the hell does that?"

"Me, most of the time. I only use force when it's the only option." He pointed at the other two men. "Might as well hear this bit of wisdom, stay a minute." Turning back to the belligerent man, he shook his head. "Talking instead of fighting should always be the first phase. Actually, if you're in a club and someone disrespects you, or you feel disrespected, the best thing is to just step away. If you're patched into an MC and you don't step away, and you're wearing your colors? You just pulled your club into a fight they didn't ask for."

"But if someone disses me, they gotta pay." This was from the second of the men who would be dismissed.

"Pay what? What do you gain if you match fist to fist with them? Winner isn't the better man, just the strongest physically. Let's say you do go to the mat with someone, and you knock them out instead of walking away. Let's say the cops are called and you get pinched? You think that's going to look good with IMC on your back? Fuck no, asshole. Now you've got to deal with *me*, in addition to dealing with the cops. See, I'm the one that gets the call when there's trouble with a member that shouldn't involve the chapter or the club. I get to sort out the headache, and then I make a recommendation to Prez. Know what those recommendation options are?"

He looked around and saw just one man with a knowing expression. "Warner, do you know?"

"Keep or cut. Those are the only two options. If you keep someone, they'll likely have to pay fines up to and in excess of whatever outlay the club had to pay on their behalf. If you cut someone, they're just gone. No arguing, no reconciliation. They are out." He grinned for a moment then the expression fell away. "My old man was in a club. Not IMC, his club doesn't exist anymore."

"Who did he ride for?" This came from one of the five who'd be staying, and Cherry liked the way they were all leaning into the exchange.

"Common Enemy MC. He's Gord. Was Gord."

"Oh, shit. I'm sorry. I heard he got sick." Cherry shook his head. "Good man, Gord. Ride in paradise. I should have made the connection."

Warner nodded. "Thanks, man. So yeah, when I told him I wanted to join, he told me to keep him out of it. It was something I had to earn on my own dime. But he wasn't shy with his knowledge. Right up to the end, he'd call me and school me on one aspect or another of the charter."

"Wish others had the same wisdom to listen." Cherry waved a hand. "You three are out of here. Go on, now." He stared from one man to the next. "I think I said, go on, now. As in get the fuck off club property and don't bother any members you see on the outside. Zebra is off limits to you now, too. You failed, and you reap the harvest."

After he'd run the rejects off, Cherry settled into his role as teacher, explaining the whys and hows of the club's expectations and rules. Running this kind of training was Pony's idea, way back when, and IMC ensured each chapter adhered to the plan. Watching as Warner rolled through question after question, he wondered if Denis could do the same.

But he isn't wanting to be a member. He is just in the bed of one.

Even old ladies of members had to adhere to a code.

Maybe I should find out what that is? Since he's a complete outsider, he's going to have questions I can't answer. Maybe I should talk to some of the old ladies. Shit, he might not want to be part. He still hasn't ridden on the bike with—

"Cherry? Enforcer? Are we done for the day?"

Cherry zoned back in and realized all five men were on their feet. "Yeah, we can be done for today. Warner, hang back a minute."

The kid hooked a toe around a chair and pulled it in front of Cherry. He waited for the other men to exit the room they were in before he sat. "Yes, Enforcer?"

"Okay, that's the right attitude." Cherry laughed. "The other day, you said you'd seen me at the club downtown."

"And I never said a word. I couldn't, not without telling on myself. Besides, every man needs to set their own course. Daddy said a few members had chapped asses about Po'Boy and his throuple, but since his patching over to the CoBos not only didn't hurt our club, but the connection also enhanced it, he didn't have a single bad thing to say about them. His counsel was 'Live and let live'."

"Good motto."

"So you wanted to make sure I wasn't going to say anything? Is that what this is?"

"No, asshole. This is me wanting to get to know you better. Gord didn't bring family around often enough. I remember a kid, must be your younger brother, but I don't remember you." Cherry blew a soft raspberry. "I hate that, but I was still in the military when you would have been coming up."

"You know everyone's family?"

"Pretty much, yeah. I wasn't kidding when I called the club 'found family.' Our bonds are much closer than blood. I trust my brothers like I trusted my men. I believe down to the soles of my boots that every man in the club will have my back. No matter what." He flexed one fist. "As Enforcer, my role is to protect and police, both within the club and environs closely managed by the club."

"Do you like the position?"

"Oh, hell yeah. It's a great fit. There's no bigger high than finding a problem and solving it to the benefit to the club."

Marcus pulled in a breath. "Have you guys heard from LaBlanc? My family?"

"Yeah, Ruger went out and talked to your mother. He also threw out that useless squatter LaBlanc from the house. It's your mom and brother there now, and we're keeping an eye on things. Scuttlebutt is that LaBlanc is trying hard to keep his numbers up, but without your information, he's failing pretty spectacularly. And before you ask, we've dealt with Caine on your behalf. He's out of the picture entirely. I wanna say he's headed to Guatemala, in a hull without a window."

"You took him out?"

"Not dead, although that might come back to bite me in the ass. No, we just sent him on a long siesta, on a slow boat. He had been junking up our town too long as it was. We've been focused on our own shit, and hadn't caught the bullshit he was bringing in."

"What will fill the vacuum? Isn't that the saying?"

"We'll be watching out for someone trying to slide in. I'm thinking of making that your first assignment."

"Y'all are patching me, then? This wasn't just for show?"

Cherry rolled his neck, groaning when it popped two or three times. "God, that feels good." Looking at Marcus, he shook his head. "Patch is yours if you want it. We wouldn't make you do shit. But if you want it, if you want to take this life on, we'll have you. Gladly."

"Cherry." A shout from the main room had them both running for the door.

"The fuck is the fire," he asked as he cleared the opening. Two men wrangled a third towards the door leading to the far back room of the clubhouse. He wasn't moving, his form sagging between the men as the toes of his boots dragged across the floor. "Who?"

"ASMC on the vest on his goddamned motherfucking back." Busk held up the confiscated colors of their biggest regional rival. "Name's Racer, which don't mean shit to me. From the colored threads on the vest, it's had a few nameplates."

"Unknown to me. Where'd you pick him up?"

"Back of the house. He brought the bike in on a cow path, stowed it about a mile away. He'd been slogging through the bayou for a while. Man's eat up with mosquito bites, too, which doesn't scream local to me."

Cherry nodded, his gaze fixed on the door, now closed, leading to the part of the clubhouse used for physical interrogation. "You call Ruger?"

"Up to you, Enforcer. Wanna bother the Prez with this?" Busk's voice didn't reflect any emotion, which had Cherry looking at him. "What?"

"What the fuck is between you and our Prez is yours to tell. But it shouldn't come into play during club business."

"Fuck!" Busk kicked out at a chair, the metal twisting as it hit the wall. "You're right, Enforcer. Thank you for calling me on my shit." He sighed. "But could you call him? I doubt he'd pick up if it was me."

"Then that's more shit of yours that needs sorted." Cherry yanked his phone out of his pocket and as he dialed Ruger's number, he caught sight of Marcus still nearby, flattened against the wall.

Shit.

The president answered with a growled, "What?"

"Ruger, we've got a tourist in our most lavish accommodations. Might want to idle this way when you can."

The call disconnected and Cherry turned to stare directly at Busk. "Shit? Your shit? Handle it."

Busk gave a jerky nod, so Cherry glanced at Marcus.

"Busk, meanwhile, get to know Marcus. His old man was Gord, something I didn't find out until today. Would have thought our intelligence man might have carried that information to our ears sooner."

"Oh, fucking shit." Busk whirled to face Marcus. "Your old man was hardcore. He was a hell of a member, loved his club, loved his family just as much. I rode escort on his funeral."

Confident Busk would keep the kid busy with his thousand-question conversation process, Cherry pushed through the door leading to the room at the back of the club, the one with a drain in the middle of the slanted floor, the one with a signal jammer, the one with hooks on the walls. The one where his work was most critical.

Life or death, yin or yang. Depends on a thousand little things.

He passed through two more doors, these with guards inside and out. The members each gave him a somber nod. They knew.

We all fucking know.

"Hold a second, Reggie," he told the outside guard on the final door. "I'm going to listen in." The room next door held speakers and a screen. He nudged the mouse to wake the computer underneath the desk, and the scene from the holding room came on screen. Adjusting the volume in tiny increments got him the verbal action, too.

"Why am I here?" That wasn't a voice he knew, and that wasn't a face he knew, which meant the ASMC was actively recruiting members. Not prospects, but members. The flayed threads around the nameplate on the vest made more sense now. That patch belonged to the club, not an individual member.

"Why do you think, asshole?" That was one of the IMC members in the room.

"I don't know, man. I don't know." That was the voice of desperation talking. *I don't buy it.*

Cherry heard three sets of footsteps, two coming towards the microphone. The man on the door opened it for them to exit. Cherry gestured them into the surveillance room.

"What did you see?"

"Stranger walking through the trees. I'd been on perimeter watch for a few hours, caught movement and zeroed in on him. Skulking like a coyote, moving tree to tree like a cartoon bandit." Salty, a member for several years, shook his head. "All the focus was front facing, which made it easy to get behind him. That's how we found the bike. He had the cut on his fucking back, out skulking on IMC land. Pissed me off, Cherry."

"How did you catch him?"

"Seriously, the man had no awareness at all. I even stepped on a stick to see if I could spook him with no luck. I had my arm around his neck before he realized what was going down." Salty pointed at the screen. "Rooster's still in there with him. He's the one who rode the bike back to the compound. He's got info on what was in the bags, and Cherry, you're gonna wanna hear about it."

"Fair." Cherry turned to the other man. "And your side of the deal?"

Bruiser, only patched for a handful of months, shook his head. "I got called in after Salty had incapacitated the asshole. I'm muscle only on this one, boss."

"Okay. Salty, can you go in and spell Rooster? Get him to come out here? Bruiser, give it five minutes and you spell Salty. I don't want anyone spending more than 5 minutes with him. I'll text Busk and get him to round up brothers to work the play. We want him thinking we've got a never-ending roster ready to go to war with one single man."

He shot a text to Busk and received a thumbs-up response. By then, Salty had gone in and Rooster had come back out to the hall. He came into the surveillance room and gave Cherry a chin lift.

"What was in the bags?"

"Serious putty. He was carrying enough C4 to blow the whole clubhouse off the map. But, and this is critical, he did not have a detonator on him or on the bike."

"Shit." Cherry tipped his head down and studied the toes of his boots for a moment. "How was it packaged?"

"M112 blocks, and I checked to see that there were sequential scan codes on them. I doubt they'd had a chance to set anything in place."

"They. Same thing I'm thinking. Someone out there has the detonators. Take half a dozen brothers and lock down the in and out access from our land. Pour another dozen into the woods. Salty saw him first, once Bruiser rotates in, get Salty to show you on the map exactly where he was. Map that back to his bike, and you'll likely find the other one. Did this guy carry a phone?"

"In the bags of the bike, opposite side to the C4."

"So he's got an understanding how the things work at least." Cherry reached for the doorknob. "Reggie, come in with me, let's sort this shit out." He glanced back. "Find the detonators."

"Ya boss," Rooster nodded.

"And make sure that serious putty is stored well away from anything we hold dear." Cherry paused. "Where's the bike?"

"Shale pit. Soon as I saw what was in there, I started the bike on that trip."

"Good call, brother. Now get out there and find the fucking detonators."

Cherry opened the door and walked through. With deliberate movements he went across the floor to where they kept a variety of stage dressing things. He picked up the whiskey bottle and took a healthy slug...of the caramel-tinted water they stored inside. In this room, he would always have the upper hand.

Need all the advantages we can buy, steal, or make.

"Racer, huh?" He stood with his back to the chair where he knew the man had been secured. "That's a name. How'd you come by it?"

"Why am I here, man?"

Cherry lifted the bottle again, taking a second long swig out of it. He hissed at the end, putting the cap back on the bottle and setting it down with a thud.

"Brother," he pointed to Bruiser, "you're spelled." Cherry watched him leave, then noted Reggie's position directly behind the intruder, and finally looked at the man currently restrained. "Racer, you're here because you were on IMC territory. We just wanna know a coupla things. Who you are, why are you here, who sent you. You know, the basics." Cherry turned slowly, holding tightly to the edge of the table as if drink was already upending his balance. "Not much, 'man'." He aimed for snide with the repeated word. "Not much."

"I didn't know for sure it was IMC. Not until I saw the clubhouse."

"But you knew it then, and you didn't immediately vacate." Cherry shrugged. "Why?" He reached back and fumbled the bottle a little, bringing it out and working at the cap, pretending to have just a little bit of problems with it. "Why would you hang around?"

"Rock and a hard place."

Cherry stared at the man, realizing he wasn't belligerent, wasn't really afraid, either. He wasn't acting or sounding like someone who understood the depth and breadth of his fuckup.

"What?" He took another swig of the colored water, clearing his throat and licking his lips, playing up the drama end of him getting a little soused while conducting an interview. The intent was always to give the person the impression that he didn't like his job, that he needed to be a little drunk to be the club's enforcer. "The fuck's that's supposed to mean?"

"I was given two long/lat locations. I went to the first and picked up three bricks of C4. This was the second location." The man laughed, the sound harsh and echoing around the room. "They didn't give me enough information, clearly."

Cherry studied him. Blood streaked his face, from a deep cut near one brow. There was also bruising on his face, and his hands bore several abrasions. He'd not come without argument. *Neither would I.* Something about the man's posture hinted at military. *That's an avenue to explore, at least.*

"Why are you here at all? What was the goal of the op?"

"There was supposed to be a well that the buyer wanted shut down for good." He worked his jaw, leaned as far to one side as he could, and spit out a mouthful of blood. *Oh, that shit's for show. He's trying to work me.* "Bike isn't mine. Too bad, she's a nice one. No well I could find, then I saw the house and decided to see what I could figure out."

"So you're not a member of the ASMC? That's interesting." Nothing was making any sense. Cherry shook his head. "Why were you wearing a vest, then?"

"Issued to me, just like the bike. And no, I'm not a member of that fucking circus." The guy spit again, the red splattering wide. "I took a job, but I'm a nonviolent contractor. I know my way around explosives, which is why I was recommended for the gig. The job I took seems to be entirely off track of what is reality." He shrugged. "I got half in advance, so at least I'm not out everything."

"What's your name?"

"Wallet was in my back pocket, one of your guys took it. My IDs are in there. I'm Manning, Chuck Manning."

"Well, Chuck Manning, I'm going to have to leave you here for a few minutes." Cherry took another swig from the bottle and pushed to his feet, fingers fumbling the lid slightly. "I'll be back." He turned to the door before looking over his shoulder, "Who was your contact in the club?"

"Apollo. He's the president. He's the money guy."

"I thought Dillinger was the money guy over there."

"I think I heard the name, but he wasn't part of the op prep."

Cherry nodded and walked through the door held open by an IMC member. "Thanks, Blackout."

The door shut behind him, and he quickly went into the room next door.

"He's not buying the booze." Busk stood next to the screen showing the inside of the room where Chuck Manning was restrained. "He's also trying to python the tape holding him to the chair. Watch him breathe in."

Cherry sighed. "Yeah, I saw that. He's subtle with everything he's doing. Trained very well. Doesn't match with the profile Salty gave of him and how they clocked him. Doesn't make sense. Did the ID confirm the name?"

"IDs, emphasis on the esss. He's well supplied with supporting documentation, but it's from too many places. It's too perfect. Why would he take real identification on a job? Smart bet is his name isn't Chuck Manning."

"No shit, Sherlock." Cherry studied the man's face on the screen. The expression was placid and calm. "Who the fuck is this goddamn icy when restrained by an unknown component. I need to shake him up."

"I don't wanna watch you do wet work, brother. I'm with you. This doesn't feel right." Busk stood and put a heavy hand on Cherry's shoulder. "But my trust in you is unwavering. The club's trust is the same."

"Denis has a PI. A good one. Ricky—"

"Ricky Parrado? He is fucking good."

"Probably. I didn't get a surname, but I've got a phone number. I think we do a couple of things fast. First, I'm going to get ahold of Ricky and get that rolling. Then, I'm going to push the guy in the room, but we get Ricky started on his documentation, too. Ideally, we'd have feedback before we have to decide to cut him loose, or take him out." Cherry looked at the screen again and caught Chuck Manning staring into the camera. "Why do you say he doesn't buy the booze?"

"He tried and failed to conceal a flash of a grin when you were acting clumsy. I don't know what tipped him off. You play that part well. I agree with the plan. Make it so." Busk looked at his watch. "I'm might not be able to be here for much longer. I've been away from home longer than I planned. Junebug is gonna roast my ass if I don't call or come home. Ruger will be here."

"Give Junie a call. I'm going to the bar and take care of the smell of booze. Maybe that was the tip-off." He shrugged. "Worth a try."

Outside in the main room of the clubhouse he noticed more members than usual were hanging around.

Salty came over. "No detonators, man. Just the C4 on the bike. No second player, either. We didn't find any prints or ruts from a second bike."

"Good news? Mixed news, maybe. How sure are we that there aren't detonators on the bike itself? Under the seat, next to the battery, under the tank? I'd say check it over with a toothpick and a mirror." He waved to the prospect manning the bar. "Shot of whiskey, man." The shot glass slammed down in front of him, filled with brown liquid. Cherry lifted it and took a sip, then another. He dipped a finger in the liquid and painted a line down the side of his throat, as if he'd missed his mouth with the first attempt.

"The fuck are you doing?" Rooster walked up behind Salty, head cocked to one side as he looked at Cherry.

"Busk thinks our guest didn't believe the booze bit. I need every edge I can get with this one, so this way I'll at least smell the part."

Both men laughed and Cherry grinned.

"Do what you gotta do, I guess." Salty lifted a finger to his brow and tipped a sassy salute. "I'll go take the bike apart, see if we missed anything."

"Says the bike isn't his, same with the cut. Send me a picture of the dismantling and I'll show him, see if that was truth." Cherry sipped a little more whiskey, then slid the glass back across the bar. "Thanks, Prospect."

Back in the room with Chuck Manning, Cherry nearly burst out laughing when he caught the man sniffing the air. He smacked his lips, and took his seat again.

"Well, Chuck." He blinked slowly. "You've got a lotta identification for a guy on a covert op. I'm a little concerned that's not your real name."

"It's my name today."

"And that, in a fucking nutshell, is the problem. Chuckie." Cherry rocked to one hip and pulled a knife from his pocket. He played with the button snapping the blade into place, popping the steel out and pushing it back into the hilt. "I'm not a fan of people pulling my leg on a whim. Thing is, you don't strike me as a guy who likes much whimsey in his life. Blood and screaming, sure. Whimsey? Nope."

"What do you want me to say?"

Cherry tipped his chin down and stared at his officer plate for a minute. Then he lifted a hand and tapped on the patch with the tip of the knife, moving his eyes to stare at Chuck Manning from underneath his brow.

Without additional prompting the man revised his question. "What do you want me to say, Enforcer?"

"There we go. That's a little respect." He sneered at Manning. "Your contact for the ASMC doesn't know shit about a Chuck Manning. Also said the cut we have in hand is one that was stolen. So ASMC you ain't, and Racer you ain't, and I'd bet the moon that Chuck Manning you ain't." He moved his jaw side-to-side. "So who and what you are is something I'm very interested in."

"I don't think you've got hold of Apollo to ask him about me." Manning breathed in deeply and Cherry watched the tape move with the shifting of the man's chest.

Nothing is loosening up that I can see. The fact he's trying it in front of me is something though.

"Oh, you don't think Apollo would pick up if I dialed? Are you fucking ignorant?" Cherry looked at his nails, beginning to clean under each with the knife. His hands were trembling slightly, not enough to get in the way of what he was doing, but just enough to hopefully sell the booze a little more. Sure enough, he saw Manning sniff quietly. *Motherfucker is subtle.*

"I don't know. With the beef between the clubs, I'd like to think he's smart enough to answer." Manning shrugged as much as he could.

Cherry's silenced phone vibrated twice against his leg which meant Ricky had called back with something he needed to know. Manning glanced at the bulge in his pocket and tipped his head to one side.

"That's something important to you. That two-pulse thing. You're quite happy to get that message. What is it, Enforcer? That message? What's it supposed to mean?"

Without engaging with Manning's questions, he stepped behind the chair. With rough hands, he tugged on the strips of tape winding around the man's torso. The makeshift restraint was still very tight, no places fraying. Cherry twisted the man's hands so they stuck out from the sides. He ignored the shouts of pain. Muscles and veins were strained in Manning's neck and his chin dropped to his chest, groaning a final time.

Cherry looked at the IMC member in the room and gestured to his eyes, then pointed to the man's hands. He got a nod in response, so he turned and stalked out of the room.

"Ricky said call, he's got the goods on this guy." Salty shook his head. "Man wouldn't give up even an ounce of what he knows. I like him already."

"Did you threaten this guy when y'all picked him up?"

"Yeah, but only about a level two threat. Next time I'll need to up my game."

Cherry snorted and walked into the nearby room, kicking the door closed behind him. He dialed, and Ricky connected the call before the first ring finished.

"John Kastle. Former FBI, former Navy, former father. That last one is most important. His little girl died a couple years ago, only child, mother gone for around fifteen years. So little is relative in this story, but remember that was his only child. She ODed, a recreational user who didn't know enough about all the shit that's flooding into our streets. Cop report said she was seen on the back of an ASMC bike the day before she was found dead. Props to Kastle, he's done his due diligence, tracked down the member, one who is missing right now, about a week ago. I know because that ASMC member left a voicemail for his president, and Apollo doesn't delete those as frequently as he should." Ricky sucked in a hard breath. "Give me two more minutes before you go in and cut him loose. That C4 was stolen from a Navy yard over by New Orleans. If it's tracked to your compound, that's a shit ton of scrutiny for you guys. I advise you get it out of there now."

"Like he's going to walk. Funny. We took it to a safe location, and we're disassembling the bike as we speak. I'm not convinced he didn't have detonators on him somehow." Cherry huffed out a sigh. "Did he ping the police about the C4?"

"Not that I can find. I just don't trust him. There's too much technical training in his background to be comfortable around him."

"You think the ASMC member is who supplied his little girl with the bad dope?"

"He thinks it was. Doesn't matter if it's true or not."

Cherry looked at the screen, watching Kastle do another of those python breaths to stretch the tape. "Lotta training in this guy."

"Yeah, makes him a little terrifying. Maybe scarier than you are, Tom."

"Fuck you, Riccardo. I'm plenty scary. You should fear."

"Oh, I do. I'm just glad I'm on the phone with you and not Kastle."

"Fair enough. Anything else you have on him?"

"Nope. John Kastle, FBI and Navy, dad to Sophea. Lives in Chicago, is not connected with the Rebels or anything up there. No idea how he came by the bike or vest."

"I figure they're both club-owned, probably lifted from storage somewhere."

"That would make sense. So that's all I got. Not a lot."

"No it fucking isn't, but it's more than I had a handful of minutes ago. You find out anything, ping me again, same pattern. I plan on staying busy with our friend for a bit." He ended the call and shoved the phone back into his pocket, still on silent. "Okay, John," he spoke to the face on the screen, "let's see what you know."

Stepping back into the interrogation room was like walking into a memory. Cherry had spent hours in the room throughout the years. It smelled of burnt coffee and old sweat, and threatened to suck the air out of anyone who overstayed their welcome. John Kastle sat in the metal chair, his broad frame dwarfing it. His eyes flicked between Cherry and the door, back to Cherry, and once the door closed there they stayed. *He expected me to bring in backup. Interesting.*

"Kastle, interesting to read about your past lives. John Kastle." The man's eyes widened for a moment, then he glanced at the bottle of caramel-colored water. "Yeah, you're right, stage dressing." He held out his hands, scarred and steady. "You're more interesting than I thought."

"Enforcer Cherry, you've got good resources."

"Oh, hell yeah. Did you think just because we're in the armpit of America we were backwards about security? Sorry to break it to you, but you're not the only smart guy in the room." Cherry grinned at the grimace Kastle couldn't hide. "I'd like to hear your side of things, Kastle. You're on IMC ground, wearing a stolen ASMC vest, riding a stolen ASMC bike, and carrying enough C4 to turn this compound into a crater. You don't get to play dumb."

Kastle's lips twitched, not quite a smirk but close enough to make Cherry's jaw clench.

"Dumb's not my style, Enforcer. You've got questions, and I've got answers. Problem is, you won't like any of them."

"John Kastle. Ex-Navy, ex-FBI, ex-father. You've been chasing shadows since your daughter overdosed, and now you're here, caught with explosives and a rival club's colors. You're not just grieving, you're a one-man wrecking crew. If Apollo isn't your contact, and isn't paying your way, then who's the bankroll behind the mask?"

John's face didn't change, but Cherry saw his fingers flex, the tight tape binding his hands out to the sides. "No bankroll, Enforcer. But mark this. Sophea's name stays out of your mouth, no matter what you think you have to say." His voice was low and controlled, but there was an edge to it, like it would flay skin upon contact.

There was a sharp rap at the door and it opened, Salty coming in and handing a fat folder to Cherry. A single nod told him all was in hand. He turned and left, the flat metallic sound of the latch engaging ringing through the room.

Cherry didn't flinch. He pulled a picture from the folder. "C4, in M112 packages." He tossed the image to the floor in front of Kastle. A picture of the vest with the frayed thread followed. "Stolen colors. You acting like a skunk ape of the swamp." A blurry shot of Kastle skulking through the bayou, caught by a trail cam. "I've got plenty more. And remember, this is where you brought all that boom, this club's house. *My* house. *My* club." He shook his head. "Right now you look exactly like a threat to everything I value. I want to know why."

"You know about my daughter. I assume you know about Beauden Smith. That's all I came to Louisiana for. I got him to tell me what happened. He carried responsibility of her death, and he owned up to everything I wanted to know. C4 isn't even connected to you. I picked that up for a different job, but I bailed on that one to get over here. Soon as I knew his name, knew who he was, I bailed."

"Stolen vest? How about that and the bike?"

"Oh, the bike is mine. I switched plates yesterday out at the truck stop. I'll put my Illinois plate back on before I leave for home."

Cherry blew a short raspberry. "Well, about that. I'm going to have some bad news here in a bit. We're still looking for detonators."

"There aren't any. You won't find any on the bike."

"Well, that's what you say. We're still gonna verify. I'm a don't trust and always verify kinda guy."

"What are they doing to Miss Maple?" Kastle glared at Cherry. "Tell me you aren't doing anything foolish."

"Man, you rode into my territory, set foot on my fucking compound, and you want to try and school me on what should and should not be done? You're full of shit." His phone buzzed and he grinned. "Fucking excellent timing." Cherry pulled his phone out and unlocked it, flipping to the message app the club used. "Oh, damn." Fairings, handlebars, seat, and saddlebags had all been removed from the body of the bike. He knew the men would take significant care of the bike, but seeing it partially disassembled would be a gut punch to Kastle.

"Show me." Kastle glared at Cherry.

"Nuh uh. You do not dictate any-fucking-thing. This here?" He flashed the screen at the man and pulled it away immediately. "Is not a leverage point for you." He pulled out a chair from the wall and settled down in front of Kastle. "Hey, I've got an idea. Tell me again where you got that C4 from? I think I've heard two different stories, and I want to get it right."

"And you'll show me Miss Maple?" Cherry watched as Kastle appeared to deflate, shoulders dropping. "Okay."

He laughed hard, throwing one hand out wide. "Jesus, can you be a little more theatrical? I think if I put in the effort on convincing you I was a drunkard you'd at least put some try into it." Cherry struck a pose, elbow on his knee. "Oh, Horatio, I knew you well."

"The line is 'Alas, poor Yorick, I knew him well'." Kastle looked down at his chest, still duct taped to the chair. "I'm not a threat here, Cherry. You've got every upper hand. I mean, you even know shit I don't tell anyone. Any chance of me getting a rest from the restraints sometime soon?"

Cherry laughed again. "Fuck no. I do not trust you as far as I could throw you. You've got a story for everything and a reason for none of it. I get what you did to the ASMC asshole. That entire club is a stain on the bayou. Trimming the fat won't upset me none." He leaned back in the chair. "If your path never crossed mine I'd be cheering you on. But you didn't roll that way. You came directly into my territory, and I'm like a pissed-off pitty when I defend my stand."

"C4 was stolen from a Navy yard in state. I'm not sure where. I really did snag it from a pickup point. The detonators were at a different location, one I never got to. I had word about the asshole who sold my little girl tainted drugs, and got her dead. So I bailed on the other job, and now I'm here. Can I see the picture of Miss Maple?"

Cherry considered. Keeping Kastle in the dark about the bike didn't further his goal of understanding why the man was here. He stood and flicked to the first image, of the bike up on a rack with parts staged around her. He showed the picture to Kastle and watched as anger rolled over his face and then was tucked away. The longer he looked at the picture the less angry he seemed.

"Half those parts aren't from Miss Maple. They're treating her with respect, even as they strip her down." Kastle shrugged. "I appreciate the care, man. She's been a good bike."

"They'll be able to put her back together, if they get the word from me." Cherry reclaimed his seat, legs sprawled out in front of him. "I'm still waiting for truth from you."

"I don't have any reason to harm anyone in an IMC vest. Or those protected by the IMC. I heard a relative of mine might be here, was going to surprise him. I vastly underestimated the security, and I'd honestly forgotten about the C4. It doesn't sweat, and as long as no form of detonator came in contact with it, I was safe as if it was a bag full of apples."

"Who? Give me a name."

"Nathan Hadley. Nate." Kastle shrugged one shoulder. "Cousin I haven't seen in forever."

"Nate Hadley is your cousin. You know I can run that line up the flagpole with a single shout. Is that your final answer?"

"Yeah, lock it in. Nate is in IMC."

Cherry leaned forwards and took a flash picture of Kastle's face. "Wonder if he'll recognize you with the warpaint." He texted the image to Busk and Ruger, and then to Salty with a request he show it to Sir Loin. He stared at Kastle, who was staring at his phone. In less than a minute, the device buzzed with an incoming message. "Well, well, let's see what he has to say." Cherry made a production of unlocking the phone and navigating to messages. "Huh. Seems you have told one truth this day." He leaned back, throwing an elbow over the seat beside him. "I'm not hearing truth with the other parts of your story, though. Gonna have to convince me." He gestured towards Kastle. "You may begin."

"Fuck, you are a hard nut to crack. Is it the Navy part that's chapped your jarhead ass? We can't all be excellent, you're punching above weight, I think. Nate gave affirmative feedback that I was known to him. Did he give me a bad review? Shit. Is he still pissed about Tanya

Greenwood? That was way back in our senior year. Get over yourself already, Nate." Kastle stared at Cherry. "That's not the name you prefer for him, is it? He's got a club name, no doubt. That I don't know, and it saddens me to no end." He slouched slightly, pulling both shoulders towards his chin.

"Will you stop trying to loosen the fucking tape? You aren't getting out of that mess without losing some hair and probably skin. Stop wiggling."

"Can't blame a man for trying."

"Fucking can. Do. Stop wiggling."

"Okay. So the C4, you can check it, the Navy has the serial numbers posted on internal boards." Kastle paused and looked sideways at Cherry. "I'm assuming you can get at that info."

"Will not confirm nor deny." Cherry thumbed a short message to Salty.

Cherry: *Get info from Ricky*

Salty: *Yas boss*

He knew they were watching the screen in the other room, knew they'd probably pulled

Sir Loin in after he'd confirmed he was the Nate Hadley, and was well acquainted with Kastle.

"Let's say I take you at your word, that you weren't aiming at any IMC members. That your only reason to be in the area is to avenge your daughter." He paused, watching Kastle's face. "How long ago did your daughter pass?"

"A day is too long. I'd always heard that parents aren't supposed to bury their children, didn't know how right it was. That bastard breathed air months longer than my baby girl, but you better believe his last breaths were imbued with all the rage in my body. I'm a big guy. I had a lotta rage."

Cherry's phone buzzed twice and he looked at the screen.

Ricky: *Checks out, and fyi ASMC is blaming IMC for the member found drowned in his own piss today*

"You drowned him in his own piss?"

Kastle's chin jerked up. "They already found him? Shit. I'm losing my touch. He shouldn't have surfaced until tomorrow at the earliest."

Ruger: *Agree to cut him loose*

Busk: *Agree to let him go*

Cherry thumbed a message in response: *Affirmative.*

He moved to a different message thread.

Cherry: *Reassemble the bike unless there's something new to report*

Salty: *Nothing of note.*

Salty: *<a picture of the bike looking good as new>*

"You just dropped about a ton of tension. All good on the outside front?" Kastle nodded at the door. "We going out that way, or am I misreading the situation?"

Cherry pulled his knife and flicked it open. Kastle's eyes flared just the barest amount.

"We going out front now?" His voice had gone up an octave.

The two strides to put Cherry at Kastle's back happened fast, taking the restrained man by surprise.

Kastle breathed out slowly. "What was the verdict, jarhead?"

Cherry ran the blade over the tape where it held his arms to his torso. The flexible material peeled back as it was sliced. "How did you know I'm Marines, frog?" He moved to the other side and made the same cuts, then stepped back a stride. "Try and move around, let's see what else I need to cut to get you outta there. Boys used most of a roll of tape, from the looks of it."

There was a loud ripping sound as the man shoved both arms out in front. He yelled and tried to pull his arms free, to no avail.

"You've got the look. Always watching. Had to be military, Marines seemed the right pick given the Semper Fi patch on your vest. Need my arms cut, at least one of them. Can you get the tape off my back?"

Cherry went around the front and sliced in the middle of the tape Kastle had pulled forwards. He then backed off again. "Nice catch with the patch. I'm done cutting, though. You'll have to get the tape. All of it. I might have gotten an order to dump you alive, but there wasn't anything about coddling you."

"Coddling, huh?" Kastle grunted as he peeled the tape off his arms. "This feels about the opposite of coddling."

"Drowned him in his own piss? How'd you even accomplish that?"

"Catheterized him for a day as I poured water down his throat. I got three liters fast. Just enough to fill up the lungs."

"Got your vengeance."

"Yup." Kastle reached behind him and yanked on the tape still attached to his back. "Gonna be a bit before I grow all my hair back." He turned around to face Cherry. "I have no ill will about anything that happened in this room. No harm, no retribution." He touched his face, fingers exploring the split skin. "Even this. I was giving them hell before they knocked me out. Now if you have some bandages or something, I wouldn't turn one down."

"We got a guy who can throw a stitch or two at that."

"Handy. You must have enough injuries to make it worth it to hire a med tech?"

Cherry laughed. "Oh, he's not a med tech, he's a member whose father was a vet. Picked up a ton of handy skills."

"Well okay then." Kastle held out the bundle of tape. "You want this?"

"Nope, you can put it in the garbage just outside the door."

"And you'll be at my back the whole way?"

"You know it. This is my club, man. My family. I'm not going to take any chances with their health and wellbeing."

"Wouldn't expect anything less, jarhead."

"Get those frog feet moving."

"Sir, yes, sir."

Outside the door Sir Loin was waiting and he smothered Kastle in a hug that looked like it released a hundred pounds of air out of the man.

"I just heard, brother. I'm so sorry. But you got him."

Cherry walked past them, hearing only mumbles after that. Salty gave him a mocking salute, and Cherry punched him hard in the arm. Busk and Ruger stood side by side on one wall of the big room and Cherry headed that direction. By the time he'd made it there, only Ruger remained. His expression seemed strained, and he had dark circles underneath his eyes.

"Prez. You've looked better. You okay? What in the hell is going on with you and Busk?"

"He had to go home. Nothing more and nothing less. I'm fine, brother. Mind your own."

"If it didn't impact the club, I would. I'm not the only one who's noticed our Prez and VP can't stand being in the same room with each other."

"Leave it, Cherry. I'm not at liberty to tell you anything else. Me and Busk are fine, no worries there. Calm the masses if you get a chance. If there's anyone else who's said something. I'm not sure but what you're the only one."

"Oh, I will pass on the message, Prez. No worries there." He paused, taking in the exhausted aura from Ruger. "You really do look like shit, brother. We help carry each other's load. If you're needing help and not asking, then you're leading with a bad example."

"It's been a rough couple of weeks, but things are going to be fine now. Maybe Busk will give you more info, but maybe not. I'm going to sleep like the dead tonight, and by tomorrow I'll be chipper as always."

"I hope to see the evidence tomorrow." Cherry glanced at the family reunion still underway. "Kastle is a cool customer. I wasn't sure about letting him walk, but now it feels like the best option. Sir Loin is a good judge of character, I'm sure he'll let us know if anything turns sour."

"Yeah, he's a good one. So are you. Nice job." Ruger looked at Cherry. "You tagged Ricky Parrado for info. He's good, I don't know why we didn't think of looping him in on some things before now. Your guy is bringing good things with him. Tell him we all approve."

"Soon as I get home, I'll tell him."

Two hours later, Cherry rolled the bike to a quiet stop outside his house. There was a light on inside, glowing brightly from the kitchen.

By the time he'd dismounted and turned for the door, it opened and Denis stood framed by the light.

"Hey there," Denis called as he made a come-here motion with his hands. "Get your fine ass over here, I'm in a kiss deficit for the day. Time to get caught up."

Cherry gladly went into his arms, finding Denis' face tipped down exactly as needed for a kiss. It started slow, a tasting, a nibble, a stroke of the tongue, then it turned into a deeper, more urgent pressing of their lips together. The kiss was nearing out of control levels when Denis pulled back. Cherry chased his mouth before pulling Denis tight against his body. They were both breathing heavily.

***

Denis

The kiss lingered in the air between them, heavy with unspoken promises. Denis leaned back, his breath uneven, eyes glinting under the porch light. Cherry's hands stayed firm on Denis' hips, anchoring him as if letting go might unravel something fragile. Two figures caught in the glow of a single bulb.

"C'mon," Denis said, his voice low, a little rough. "Let's clean you up and head out. I've got plans for us tonight."

Cherry raised an eyebrow, loosening his grip but not stepping away. "Plans? You gonna surprise me with a candlelit dinner or some romantic shit?"

Denis laughed, his joy bright and unforced. "Maybe I am. You got a problem with that?"

"Nah," Cherry said, smirking. "Just didn't think you'd pick talking over a club."

"There's a lot you don't know about me, Tattoo." Denis winked, tugging Cherry inside. The kitchen was warm, cluttered with books, a half-empty coffee pot, and the faint smell of something grilled: Denis' lunch. Cherry's place was lived-in, chaotic, a stark contrast to Denis' house. He lived there, but didn't really leave an impression.

Unless Cherry's there. Then it feels like home.

He brushed the thought away. Tonight's dinner would be telling, finding out if they had a connection deeper than the physical.

That physical link between us is so, so good.

They got ready quickly, Cherry rinsing road dust from his face while Denis swapped his tee for a dark button-up he knew played off the color of his eyes. He caught Cherry staring and stepped close, resting a hand on Cherry's chest as he balanced to slide on his shoes. He allowed himself to be drawn to Cherry's easy intensity, then shoved the feeling down.

Focus on the night.

An hour later, they were at a small Italian restaurant, tucked in a quiet corner of the city. The place was intimate, low lights and close tables. Denis had picked it, wanting a place to talk, not just lose themselves in the moment. Cherry, still in his leather jacket, looked a little rough against the white tablecloths, but Denis didn't care. Cherry was across from him, listening closely as Denis spoke animatedly, describing a street mural he'd seen last week.

"It was wild," Denis said, twirling spaghetti on his fork. "This huge wall, all these jagged colors, like the artist was fighting something. Reminded me of you today, actually. With all the mess around Kastle."

"You think I should've killed him?" Cherry asked, voice low, edged with something sharp. "Kastle's slick as a snake. He'd have slipped any cage we put him in. We don't cage people."

Denis leaned back, keeping his gaze steady on Cherry. "I'm not saying you should've hauled him to the cops, Cherry. But...I don't know. Letting him go? After everything he pulled? It feels like you're left cleaning up his mess. Will the ASMC care that the IMC is sheltering someone they'd like to end? Is there danger for you or the club?"

Cherry set his bottle down, the clink sharp against the table. "You weren't there, Denis. He wasn't bullshitting about anything. Ricky was able to verify everything, including the body they found today. Kastle isn't a danger to the club. It feels black and white to me."

Denis' jaw tightened, but his voice stayed even. "That's the difference between us, isn't it? You cut things off, keep it practical. Me? I can't stop thinking there's gotta be consequences, or something like it. Kastle could have burned everyone, and letting him walk feels like lady justice has been shortchanged."

Cherry's eyes flashed, irritation flaring. "I'm here, Denis. I spent my day tearing into Kastle, digging up his lies, and I still showed up for this damn dinner. I could be out there, riding off steam, but I'm trying it your way. Don't make it sound like I'm not in this. I'm here."

Denis leaned forwards, voice low but intense. "I'm not saying you're not in it. I'm saying you don't hope for more. You deal with what's in front of you, and that's it. I want us to be bigger than that. Bigger than any ASMC fallout. I want us to build something, not just survive it."

***

Cherry

The words stung, stirring something in Cherry he didn't want to name. Denis' idealism was maddening, but it was one of the things that drew Cherry in, the fire that made Denis burn brighter than anyone. He wanted to argue, to tell Denis to stop chasing dreams, but his throat tightened. Instead, he reached across the table, grabbing Denis' hand, his grip firm, steady.

"I'm here," Cherry said, quieter now. "I don't know about justice or 'consequences,' but I'm with you. That's something."

Denis' expression softened, his thumb brushing over Cherry's knuckles. "Yeah. It's a lot."

They didn't resolve it, not fully. The tension hung between them, taut but not snapping. They finished dinner in a quieter rhythm, trading lighter stories, letting the weight settle. When they stepped outside, the night was colder, streetlights casting long shadows across the pavement.

They walked in silence, shoulders brushing, until Denis stopped under a flickering streetlight. He turned to Cherry, his face half-lit, half-hidden. "You're still with me, right?"

Cherry didn't answer with words. He stepped close, cradling Denis' face, and kissed him. It was slower than their earlier kiss, more deliberate, and felt like a quiet promise. Denis leaned into it, hands tightening on Cherry's waist, and for a moment, the world was just them, him and Denis wrapped in the unsteady glow.

When they parted, Denis gave a small, real smile. "Okay. That's enough for now."

Cherry nodded, his hand lingering on Denis' cheek. "Yeah. For now."

They walked on, unresolved but tethered, the night stretching out like a road they'd figure out together.

Chapter Eighteen

Cherry

Several long weeks later, the ASMC finally struck back. They claimed responsibility for a torched warehouse on the edge of Baton Rouge, where IMC rented storage for bike parts and supplies. Ruger called it "a blazing middle finger to the idea of a truce or understanding."

It took a day, but Cherry found where their leadership had holed up and sent out an all-hands call, with a rally point a few miles from the true location, a bar. He kept an open line with the bartender, handset laid on the countertop so he could listen in on the loud bragging the ASMC was doing.

Within twenty minutes, they had enough members at the meeting place, so Cherry sent out another all-hands text, pointing everyone to the bar.

With tension high they mounted up, and he rode out knee-to-knee with Busk; Denis' worried *Stay safe* text burning in his pocket. The fight was quick and brutal. IMC had brought only fists and chains, leaving an ASMC prospect the first one spitting blood and teeth. Cherry pushed hard to make ASMC scatter, and he smiled when they left the bar via four different doors. Each man's only thought was their individual safety. He chased the VP out to the lot and caught up to him just before he swung a leg over a bike. Cherry didn't announce himself, just swung the length of chain at the man's legs, taking them out from under him. The man howled, rolling to his back with hands up defensively.

"The fuck, man?" The lack of eloquence made Cherry laugh.

"Reminding all of you to stay clear of the IMC, because we'll go hard next time. Scatter your bones in a dozen bayou. You want to convince your president to relocate, or I'll keep hunting you."

Cherry took a hit to the ribs and swung around to find two ASMC members standing there with only bare fists. He threatened with the chain and both broke, bolting away without a word.

"They don't give a shit about anything." Cherry probed the growing lump along his ribcage. "They also aren't any use in a fight, but I suspect you're realizing that now."

The man clawed his way upright and gestured to the bike. Cherry nodded, advising, "Might wanna have someone give me a shout when you've worked out your plan. We'll hit you again, and the next time we'll be playing hardball." The VP nodded and climbed aboard the bike. In less than a minute, he was gone up the dirt road, not even looking back at the five or six members laid out in the grass.

"He's a shit officer." Cherry turned, Busk walking up. Together they surveyed the little bit of damage given to the IMC members. They'd taken a few hits, but gave worse, and as the dust settled, the line held.

It would be up to the presidents of the clubs to sort out a truce, or the next lesson the ASMC learned would be a final one for many of them.

"Good job, Enforcer. Your intelligence was completely spot on." Busk turned as more IMC members rolled to a stop in the bar's lot. "I think I need to buy a couple of rounds for the locals and our guys. That way they'll get the stories told, letting them expand from there."

"Sounds like a good plan. I'm going to check the ones still down, figure out what we're going to do with them." Cherry shook his head. "Hopefully they can all ride out. That'd be better than me rounding up a few cages."

"You get done with that, come inside and get a beer. Celebrate with your brothers."

"Yes, sir." Cherry grinned at him, still riding the high of the successful operation. "See you in a few, brother."

Back at Denis' place that night, bruised and still buzzing with adrenaline, Cherry let Denis patch him up. The man's hands were gentle, but the look in his eyes fierce. "You're insane," Denis muttered, but his kiss was hungry, claiming, and Cherry sank into it, the tension bleeding out of his muscles.

Hands roaming up and down Denis' sides, Cherry let himself relax for the first time.

"Not running," Cherry said against his lips, echoing that first night.

Denis smiled, sharp and sure. "Not letting you."

"You done playing Nightingale nurse?" Cherry gripped Denis' hips and rolled them, landing on top of Denis. "Because we could do some other roleplay if you wanted." He ground his hips against Denis' and found a matching erection. Groaning, he urged, "Tell me you're ready."

"Well, it'll take a little work …"

"I can put in the work, my guy. Long as you're ready to start now." Cherry leaned in for another kiss. It was so good he sought out another that was slower, longer, and somehow hotter. "God, Denis, you just do it for me."

"Backatcha." Denis nuzzled close, brushing against Cherry's lips in a way that seemed to set every atom on fire.

Hands brushed the front of Cherry's pants and he pulled back to accommodate Denis' seeking fingers. Those same fingers quickly wrapped around Cherry's cock and stroked slowly. "God." Cherry let his eyes close, straining to hold still as Denis played. Then the heat and pleasure went away and Cherry's eyes snapped open to see Denis fumbling with the drawer of the coffee table.

"Dammit." The drawer pulled out, spilling everything on the floor. "We need to move this to the bedroom. And remind me later to restock our supplies." Denis leaned up and pressed a kiss to Cherry's lips. "Because spontaneity apparently needs planning."

Cherry laughed as he moved, and reached for Denis' hand to pull him upright. "Planned or not, get your ass to the bedroom, my Guy. I want to love on you."

"You do not need to tell me twice, baby."

Cherry slipped an arm around Denis' waist. "Come on, my Guy." He paused and looked up at Denis. "You gotta tell me if I'm pressing past any kind of line you might have, Denis." He swallowed and heard his throat click, a dryness there that hadn't been present throughout the entire fight tonight. "I'm pulling you into my world pretty fast. Let me know if we need to do more talking, or slow down, or anything." Closing his eyes, he burst out, "Fuck! Why is this so goddamned hard?"

"Because it matters." Denis pressed a kiss against Cherry's temple. "Because life is hard and real, and in our face. And sometimes bloody." He pulled back and Cherry was looking up into his eyes. "Did I tell you I finally asked Judge Cooper about the tape recorder in the PD's room?" Cherry shook his head. "He claimed no knowledge, and took me down to the room ASAP to check it out. The set-up was gone."

"Dammit, who would have had time to yank things out?"

"Me."

Cherry felt his eyes get round. "You? What the fuck?"

"I have pictures of the illegal tape station, but if I need to, I can surface the actual tape and device. There are some interesting conversations that happened in that room." Denis grinned, spreading his feet as he pulled Cherry close. "The look on Cooper's face was telling, because he didn't know about it. There was no fear or anger at it being gone. He probably is still waiting for the punchline of a joke I wasn't making."

"Interesting. If not him, then who?"

"I've got my suspicions, and right up there is the state AG wannabe. The main bailiff is his cousin on his momma's side, and they're thick as thieves." Denis leaned in and captured Cherry's mouth, his eyes fluttering closed. "Now, where were we?"

Cherry angled his jaw, inviting more of Denis' attention. "Let's get headed to the bedroom, my Guy. Let's set the world aside and celebrate the good guys winning one today."

"Agree you're a good guy." Denis caught another kiss before turning to lead Cherry to the bedroom. "Agree you're my guy."

"Maybe we're each other's guy?" Cherry let their arms stretch out, his focus on the way their hands slotted together. "I think that's the most plausible thing. We both found what we wanted, and it happens to be with each other."

***

A week later, Cherry noticed how the city lights flickered through the window of

Denis's living room, casting a soft glow across the hardwood floor where he stood, still clad in his leather motorcycle jacket. The ride from tonight's bar had been exhilarating. Cherry enjoyed weaving his bike through the late-night streets, Denis's arms wrapped tightly around his waist, the lawyer's chest pressed against his back. The vibration of the engine, the cool night air, and the heat of Denis's body had left Cherry buzzing with anticipation. Now, inside the quiet of Denis's upscale house, that buzz felt like a live wire sparking between them.

Cherry unzipped his jacket, letting it hang open to reveal a tight black T-shirt that clung to his lean, muscled frame. He was all rough edges, nothing soft about him. From the calloused hands earned by wrenching bikes, to a faint scar on his jaw from a bar fight years ago, and a smirk that promised trouble.

Denis, in contrast, was polished as always, his tailored shirt slightly rumpled from the ride, his dark hair mussed just enough to hint at the man beneath the lawyer's facade.

What they had was still so new. In terms of time, it had been just a handful of dates and late-night texts building something fragile but potent. No confessions of love, no grand promises...yet. But in terms of emotional connection, there was just a shared understanding that they were drawn to each other in ways neither could quite explain.

"Drink?" Denis asked, his voice low, almost cautious, as he closed the door behind them. He stood close enough that Cherry could smell his cologne, the scent hinting at something crisp and expensive, undercut by the faintest trace of sweat from their ride.

Cherry shook his head, stepping closer, his boots heavy on the floor. "Don't need it," he said, his voice carrying the gravel of too many whiskey shots and late nights. "Got enough of a buzz already." His hand reached out, fingers grazing the collar of Denis's shirt, the fabric smooth under his rough touch.

Denis caught his wrist, his grip firm but gentle, and brought Cherry's hand to his lips. He kissed the knuckles, his eyes locked on Cherry's, dark and searching. "What do you want, then?" The question was a challenge, an invitation wrapped in velvet.

"You," Cherry said, the word simple but heavy with intent. He closed the distance, their lips meeting in a kiss that was soft at first, more an exploratory expedition. Cherry's hands framed Denis's face, thumbs brushing over the faint stubble along his jaw. The pressure of Denis's arms slid around Cherry's waist, pulling him closer until their bodies pressed together, the leather of Cherry's jacket creaking softly.

The kiss deepened, slow and deliberate, like they were savoring the taste of each other. Cherry's tongue traced the seam of Denis's lips, coaxing them open, and Denis responded with a quiet moan, his tongue meeting Cherry's in a languid dance. The world narrowed to the immediate moment. He focused on the warmth of their mouths, the slight hitch in Denis's breath, the way his fingers tightened in his Guy's hair. It was intimate, unhurried, a tableau where time seemed to pause.

Denis pulled back just enough to trail kisses along Cherry's neck, his lips finding the pulse point beneath his ear. Cherry tilted his head, giving him better access, a soft sigh escaping him as Denis nipped lightly at the sensitive skin. "You smell like the road," Denis murmured, his breath hot against Cherry's throat. "Leather and gasoline."

"Complaining?" Cherry's voice was teasing, but there was a vulnerability beneath it, a question he didn't voice.

"Never." Denis pushed the jacket off Cherry's shoulders, letting it fall. Cherry caught it before it hit the floor, folding it reverently with the patch on the top of the bundle. Denis's fingers traced the hem of Cherry's shirt, slipping just beneath to graze the warm skin of Cherry's abdomen.

Cherry's breath caught, and he tugged at Denis's tie, loosening the knot with deft fingers. "This thing's gotta go," he muttered, tossing the silk aside. His hands worked quickly on the buttons of Denis's shirt, revealing smooth skin and the faint definition of his chest. Cherry's palms slid over Denis's shoulders, pushing the shirt off, his touch lingering as if memorizing every inch.

They moved to the couch in a slow, almost choreographed dance, their lips finding each other again and again. Denis sat first, pulling Cherry onto his lap. Cherry straddled him, knees sinking into the cushions, their bodies aligned in a way that felt both new and familiar. Their kisses were still slow, exploratory, but there was a growing heat between them, a promise of more.

Cherry's hands roamed Denis's shoulders and arms, feeling the play of muscles under his skin. Denis's fingers dug into Cherry's hips, guiding him as they rocked together gently, the friction of their jeans sending sparks through both of them. "You're gonna kill me," Denis whispered against Cherry's lips, his voice rough with want.

"Good way to go," Cherry shot back, his smirk audible. He ground down harder, drawing a groan from Denis. The movement was deliberate, teasing, building the tension like a slow-burning fuse.

Denis's hands slipped under Cherry's shirt, pushing it up and over his head. The cool air hit Cherry's skin, raising goosebumps, but Denis's mouth was there, kissing a path down his chest. He lingered at Cherry's nipples, sucking gently, his tongue flicking over the sensitive buds. Cherry's head fell back, a low moan vibrating in his throat. "Fuck, Denis," he breathed, his hands threading through Denis's hair, holding him close. "So good, Denis. So fucking good."

They took their time, exploring each other with hands and mouths, learning the contours of desire. Denis's fingers traced the scars on Cherry's torso, each one a remnant of a life lived hard and fast. Cherry's hands mapped Denis's body, memorizing the dip of his collarbone, the curve of his biceps. There was a tenderness to it, a quiet intimacy that spoke of something deeper than lust, though neither named it.

"Tell me if it's too much," Denis said, his voice soft as his hand slid lower, cupping Cherry through his jeans.

Cherry's laugh was low, husky. "It's perfect. Keep going."

Denis's fingers worked the button of Cherry's jeans, popping it open and tugging the zipper down. He pushed the denim aside, his hand slipping inside to stroke Cherry through his briefs. Cherry's hips bucked, a sharp intake of breath escaping him. "Yeah, like that," he murmured, his voice thick.

They shed their clothes piece by piece, the act a slow unveiling. Denis's pants hit the floor, followed by Cherry's jeans, until they were both bare, skin against skin. They moved to the floor, the rug soft beneath them, their bodies entwined. Denis hovered over Cherry, his eyes searching, as if asking permission one last time.

Cherry pulled him down, kissing him fiercely. "I want you," he said, the words raw and honest.

Denis nodded, reaching for a condom and a bottle of lube from a nearby drawer. He coated his fingers, his touch gentle as he prepared Cherry, his movements slow and careful. Cherry's breath hitched, his body relaxing under Denis's touch, the intimacy of the act grounding them both. When Denis entered him, it was slow and deliberate, each inch a careful exploration. Cherry groaned, his hands gripping Denis's shoulders, urging him closer.

They moved together, their rhythm unhurried, savoring the connection. Denis's thrusts were deep, measured, each one drawing a soft moan from Cherry. They kissed through it, lips and tongues tangling, their breaths mingling. Cherry's legs wrapped around Denis's waist, pulling him deeper, their bodies finding a rhythm that felt like a conversation filled with a communal give and take, push and pull.

Cherry's thoughts drifted as they moved, a mix of sensation and emotion. He'd never expected this. Couldn't have foretold how Denis, with his sharp suits and sharper mind, fit so perfectly against him. They were opposites in so many ways, yet here, in this moment, they were one. He felt the potential for love, a seed planted but not yet named, and it thrilled and terrified him in equal measure.

The pace began to shift, the smoldering heat giving way to something more urgent. Cherry's hands roamed Denis's back, nails digging in as he urged, "Faster."

Denis complied, his thrusts quickening, the slow burn igniting into a blaze. The room filled with the sounds of their bodies. Sweaty skin slapping, breaths ragged, and low moans growing louder. Cherry's hips met each thrust, his body arching, chasing the pleasure building in his core.

"Denis. Please, fuck, don't stop," Cherry gasped, his voice breaking.

Denis's response was a low growl, his movements becoming erratic, driven by need. They were frantic now, bodies slamming together, sweat slicking their skin. Cherry's hand slid between them, stroking himself in time with Denis's thrusts, the dual sensation pushing him towards the edge.

When it hit, it was overwhelming. Cherry's orgasm ripping through him, his body clenching around Denis as he cried out. Denis followed moments later, his release spilling inside the condom, his groan muffled against Cherry's neck.

They collapsed together, breathless and spent, limbs tangled on the rug. Cherry's chest heaved, his heart pounding as Denis's weight settled against him, a comforting pressure. They lay there in silence, the city's hum a distant backdrop to their shared breathing.

Denis cock slipped free, causing them both to groan. "I gotta take care of the condom."

"In a minute." Cherry chuckled softly, his voice rough. "You're gonna have to carry me to bed after that."

Denis laughed quietly, pressing a soft kiss to Cherry's shoulder. "I'll gladly admit that you've wrecked me." He shifted and grunted, and Cherry felt the back of his hand against his splattered stomach. "There, condom, done."

They stayed like that, basking in the afterglow. Cherry knew love wasn't there yet, but it was close, a promise in the way they held each other. His fingers traced lazy patterns on Denis's chest as they lay still, the rug soft beneath them but not quite enough to keep the chill of the floor at bay. "Bed?" Cherry suggested, his voice low, teasing.

Denis nodded, pulling Cherry to his feet. They detoured to the bathroom for a quick clean-up, and then stumbled to the bedroom, hands never leaving each other, their laughter soft in the quiet house. The bed was a haven of crisp sheets, and the faint scent of Denis's cologne. They fell onto it, bodies entwining once more, the night far from over.

Denis kissed Cherry slowly, his lips lingering, as if memorizing the shape of his mouth. Cherry responded in kind, his hands sliding up Denis's back, fingers digging into the muscle there. The smoldering heat returned, a slow build that felt like a continuation rather than a restart. Denis's hand found Cherry's hip, pulling him closer, their bodies aligning perfectly.

"You're addictive," Denis murmured, his lips brushing Cherry's ear.

Cherry grinned, nipping at Denis's jaw. "Good. 'Cause I'm not done with you yet."

They explored each other still, hands and mouths mapping familiar territory with new reverence. Denis's fingers traced the scars on Cherry's ribs, his touch gentle, curious. "These tell stories," he said softly.

"Some good, some not," Cherry replied, his voice quiet. He didn't elaborate, and Denis didn't push for more information, making the moment feel significant, a sharing of trust.

Denis's mouth moved lower, kissing a path down Cherry's chest, lingering at his navel before continuing south. He took Cherry in his mouth, slow and deliberate, his tongue swirling in patterns that made Cherry's hips buck. "Fuck, Denis," Cherry groaned, his hands fisting the sheets.

Denis took his time, drawing out the pleasure, his movements unhurried but precise. Cherry's moans grew louder, his body trembling under the onslaught. When Denis added a finger, curling it just right, Cherry's back arched, a sharp cry escaping him.

But Cherry wasn't content to just receive. Once the tremors abated, he pulled Denis up, flipping their positions so he was on top. "My turn," he said, his voice a low growl. He kissed his way down Denis's body, taking him in his mouth with the same deliberate care Denis had shown. Denis's hands gripped Cherry's hair, his moans filling the room as Cherry worked him, slow and teasing.

The pace shifted again, the smoldering giving way to frenzy. Cherry quickly slipped a condom down the length of Denis' cock, then straddled Denis, guiding him inside with a groan. They moved together, fast and hard, the bed creaking under their weight. Cherry's hands braced on Denis's chest, his hips rolling in a rhythm that drove them both wild.

"Cherry. Oh my God, Cherry. Holy fuck, you're gonna kill me," Denis gasped, his hands gripping Cherry's thighs.

"Worth it," Cherry panted, his movements relentless.

They chased their release together, bodies slick with sweat, breaths ragged. When it came, it was explosive, their cries mingling as they collapsed in a heap.

In the quiet aftermath, Cherry nestled into Denis's side, his head on his chest. The words he couldn't say hung in the air, but he didn't need them, not yet. This was enough, a beginning that promised more.

He woke hours later, the city was still dark outside. Cherry's hand found Denis's under the sheets, their fingers intertwining telling him Denis was awake too.

"You're still here," Denis murmured, his voice sleepy but warm.

"Where else would I be?" Cherry replied, his tone light but his grip tightening.

They made love again, slower this time, a gentle exploration that felt like a promise. Cherry believed each touch, each kiss was a step towards something deeper, a future where love might be spoken aloud. Where Denis would be his Guy forever.

Chapter Nineteen

Cherry

The sun hung low over the Louisiana skyline, casting long shadows across the cracked asphalt of the Incoherent clubhouse lot. Cherry straddled his bike, the beast rumbling beneath him like a caged animal eager for the hunt. His cut felt heavier than usual today, weighted down by the fresh insult from those Azrael's Scimitars motherfuckers.

The ASMC had crossed a line, tagging their territory with spray-paint slurs that hit too close to home, mocking the club's colors and whispering rumors about weaknesses in the ranks. Cherry's jaw clenched as he revved the engine, the vibration shooting up his arms, grounding him in the moment.

Cherry killed the engine and swung off the bike, boots crunching gravel as he headed inside. The clubhouse was a fortress of faded glory: pool tables scarred from too many games, walls plastered with photos of brothers lost and rides eternal. As always, when there was tension in the club, the air smelled of cigarettes and stale beer, the faint whang of motor oil riding the air. He nodded at a dozen men, getting a "brother" back from many. The others returned his chin lift, worry on their expression. In the back room, the war council waited.

IMC patch on his back was a badge of honor, but today it felt like a target. IMC had been through hell and back, but the latest slap from the ASMC had the whole chapter buzzing with rage.

Cherry's boots thudded on the worn wooden floor as he made his way to the back room. Voices murmured behind the door, deep, gravelly tones laced with anger. He pushed it open, nodding to the men inside.

Wildman dominated the space, his broad shoulders straining against his cut. As president of the mother chapter, he carried the weight of the entire club on those shoulders. His beard was a wild tangle of gray and black, eyes piercing like daggers. "Cherry," he said, voice like thunder rolling in from afar. "Sit your ass down. We got business."

Ruger, the chapter president, sat to Wildman's right, his face a mask of controlled fury.

Named for the gun he always carried, Ruger was the strategist, the one who turned chaos into plans. His arms were crossed, revealing tattoos that told stories of battles won and lost.

Busk paced the room, cigarette dangling from his lips. The VP was a live wire, always moving, always ready for a fight. Scars crisscrossed his knuckles, souvenirs from enforcing club law. "Those ASMC bastards think they can piss on our turf?" he snarled. "Tagging our fence with that fairy shit? And jumping Rooster? It's war."

Cherry took his seat, leaning forwards. "What'd they hit him with?"

"Knife," Ruger said flatly. "Busted rib, but he's patching up. Says it was three of 'em, wearing ASMC colors. This ain't the first insult, but it's the boldest."

Wildman slammed a fist on the table, making the ashtrays jump. "We don't let this slide. Last time they encroached on our run routes, we let it go with a warning. No more. We hit their last stash house. Torch it to the ground."

The room fell silent for a beat, then nods all around. Cherry's pulse quickened. Retaliation was the lifeblood of the club. It would always be eye for an eye, fire for fire. But something twisted in his gut. Denis. The thought of his boyfriend waiting for him, that dinner date they'd planned for weeks. Denis, with his pressed suits and sharp mind, who saw the world in shades of justice and law, not blood and brotherhood.

They dove into the plan. The stash house was a dilapidated warehouse on the edge of town, stocked with ASMC's illicit goods such as meth, guns, whatever they peddled to fund their operations. Intelligence from a hangaround had pinpointed it, the location was lightly guarded, with easy access from the back roads.

"Cherry, you lead the ride," Wildman decided. "Pick your team. Fifteen brothers, no more. Keep it tight."

Cherry nodded. "Salty for lookout, he's got eyes like a hawk. Sir Loin for muscle; guy's built like a tank. Jinx for distractions; his bad luck is our good fortune. Doodle for maps; he knows every back alley. And Rooster, if he's up for it. Wounded or not, he's family."

Busk grinned. "Rooster's already gearing up. Says the pain fuels him."

They mapped it out: approach at dusk, with a silent infiltrate. Each member had two Molotovs to ignite, and then they were to exfil before the flames drew attention. No kills if avoidable. Wildman was adamant about that. "We ain't murderers," he said. "But we are IMC. We protect what's ours."

As the meeting broke, Cherry stepped outside for air. The lot was alive with brothers prepping bikes, the hum of engines a symphony. He pulled out his phone, staring at Denis' contact photo, a candid shot of him laughing, tie askew after a long day in court.

Fingers hesitated, then typed: *Babe, club stuff came up. Gonna be late for our date. Hate letting you down. You mean the world to me. Much more than I say.* He hit send, heart in his throat. Deeper feelings. Yeah, that was as close as he got. Denis was queer, out, and unapologetic, a beacon in Cherry's shadowed world. Denis saw the man, not the biker. But how long could that last with nights like this?

A reply buzzed in: *Understand. Be safe. Miss you too.* Simple, but it warmed him.

"Ready, brother?" Busk called, mounting his bike.

Cherry pocketed the phone. "Born ready."

The ride out was electric. Fifteen bikes in formation, Cherry at the point, wind tearing at his cut. Salty rode left flank, Sir Loin right, Jinx and Doodle in the pack, Rooster bringing up rear with a grimace but steady throttle. The road wound through fields and forgotten towns, the setting sun painting everything gold and red.

Adrenaline pumped, masking the doubt that lurked like a shadow. *Was this worth it?* The club was family, but Denis was...home. The thought of losing him to this life gnawed at Cherry, but the roar of the bikes pushed it down.

They stashed the rides a half-mile out, hiking through brush. The warehouse loomed, dim lights inside, ASMC prospects lounging out front. One was half turned away, but the profile looked familiar. Cherry leaned forwards, trying to see the face on the man. All he could make out was a set of initials on the prospect's vest: HL

Cherry signaled that they were a go. In response, Salty and Sir Loin circled, each taking out a guard with a quiet chokehold. Then Jinx created the diversion they needed, his thrown rock drawing the remaining ASMC man's eyes. Doodle handed out the last few bottles, rag wicks soaked in gas.

"Now," Cherry whispered.

Flames leaped as the Molotovs shattered windows. Shouts erupted, but the IMC was already melting into the night. Bikes thundered to life as they retreated, fire reflecting in rearview mirrors. Adrenaline masked the doubt, but deep down, Cherry knew that this life, this fire, it was consuming him too.

Back at the clubhouse, beers flowed, backs slapped. But Cherry slipped away, texting Denis: *On my way.* The adrenaline faded, doubt creeping back. Maybe it was time for change.

Cherry's mind wandered as he rode. He remembered the first time with Denis, those stolen kisses on a dance floor, the contrast of soft hands on rough skin. Saying goodbye, Denis had whispered, "You're not just a biker to me." But club life demanded loyalty, and tonight proved it.

Chapter Twenty

Denis

The judge stared at the prosecutor with a steely gaze, his patience clearly thinning. He'd already made it clear he expected precision in his courtroom. Denis felt a pang of sympathy for McKinney, but the prosecution had brought this case, and they'd have to deal with the consequences.

"Mr. McKinney, can you explain in ten words or less why the arresting officer isn't present to deliver his testimony?" The judge's tone was sharp, and Denis winced, knowing the officer's absence was a critical misstep in a case hinging on conflicting accounts.

McKinney stood, adjusting his tie. "Officer LaBlanc was injured in a fire, Your Honor."

Denis's ears perked up. A few days ago, Cherry had come home reeking of kerosene and smoke, brushing it off as "club business." Denis had scoured the news and found reports of a warehouse fire, cause unknown, with police claiming they had very little information. If that warehouse tied to ASMC and LaBlanc was there, it was a connection even Ricky hadn't caught.

"What does this all mean?" Marcus Warner whispered, leaning close. "I don't get it. They've got the paperwork."

"If the officer can't testify, their case weakens," Denis murmured, squeezing Marcus's hand. "Let's see how this plays out."

"Mr. McKinney, can you proceed without the officer, or do you need a recess to contact him?" The judge leaned forwards, his expression expectant.

McKinney cleared his throat, gripping his notes. "Your Honor, we request a brief continuance to verify Officer LaBlanc's availability. His report and body cam footage can substantiate the charges, and we have secondary witnesses prepared to testify."

Denis rose, seizing the moment. "Your Honor?"

The judge nodded. "Yes, Mr. Chapin?"

"I move to dismiss the charges. The prosecution's case relies heavily on Officer LaBlanc's testimony. This is the third delay due to his absence, violating my client's right to a speedy trial under the Sixth Amendment. Without him, their evidence lacks foundation."

The judge turned to McKinney. "Response, Mr. McKinney?"

McKinney straightened, his voice firm. "Your Honor, a dismissal is premature. Officer LaBlanc's report is admissible, and our other witnesses can establish the events. We ask for a 24-hour recess to confirm his condition or proceed with existing evidence."

The judge considered, tapping his pen. "Mr. Chapin, you've claimed a speedy trial violation. Can you substantiate the prejudice to your client?"

Denis kept his tone steady. "Your Honor, these repeated delays have kept Mr. Warner under bond for months, disrupting his life. The officer's absence undermines our ability to cross-examine the primary witness, violating his Sixth Amendment rights."

The judge's eyes narrowed. "Mr. McKinney, I'm concerned about the pattern of delays. However, I'll grant a 24-hour recess to confirm the officer's status. If he's unavailable and no sufficient alternative evidence is presented, I'll entertain the motion to dismiss, potentially with prejudice. We'll reconvene tomorrow at 10 a.m."

McKinney nodded, his jaw tight. "Understood, Your Honor."

Denis gathered his papers, gesturing for Marcus to rise. "Come on, Marcus, let's prep for tomorrow."

"What's 'with prejudice' mean?" Marcus asked, tugging at his unfamiliar tie.

"It means if the judge dismisses, they can't refile the same charges. But we're not there yet. Stay clean, and let the club know you might need their support for a fresh start."

***

Cherry

"Hang on," Cherry told Busk, "my Guy is calling."

"Man has a name, brother."

"Get away from me." He put the answered phone up to his ear, grinning when he heard loud laughter over the call. "How's my Guy?"

"Who were you having to beat off with a stick? Should I be jealous?" Denis' voice carried a strong thread of laughter still. "Oh, oh. Don't tell me. Let me guess." A pause with more laughter. "Um. Oh, I know. Jinx. Was it Jinx?"

"No. Busk was being annoyingly attached." Cherry grinned at the shout of mock rage from across the room. "Might need to get some surgery to get him off my...I'm going to stop right there."

"You are the most amazing man I know." There was noise in the background, a voice asking a question. "Yes, it's Cherry. Did you want to talk to him?" A pause. "Okay."

Muffled sounds then Warner's voice came on the line. "I don't know if Chapin picked up on it, but that rookie LaBlanc missed court today because he got burned a few nights ago. Are you thinking what I'm thinking?"

"If you're thinking that my Guy missed that little tidbit, then you have no faith in him. I'll bet you ten dollars he was going to tell me tonight. But yeah, the other thinking I'm doing is that it is an interesting coincidence. Far as you know, has your cousin ever hung out with the ASMC?"

"No, but I've been ducking him for years. There are whole swaths of years when I wouldn't have to put up with his shit."

"No worries. Give the phone back to Denis. We'll sort out what might be going on."

More muffled sounds, then Denis spoke, his tone put-upon, "I did catch that little tidbit. It's why—" He sighed. "Know what? Never mind, I know I was going to tell you, and if all Marcus is going to do is mock me, then I'll leave it." In a whisper, Denis said, "But I was going to tell you."

"I believe you, baby. You're the smartest man I know." Cherry got a glimpse of his own face in the mirror behind the bar and paused to study the reflection. *I look softened, and happy.*

"So we called for a dismissal and I think it's a good chance of getting one. LaBlanc is the only witness that's not second hand. His bodycam footage doesn't prove anything one way or another. I think the judge is going to allow the dismissal as a kick in the ass to the rookie. Maybe he's had to deal with him on other cases, too."

"Did you call Ricky about the potential link between LaBlanc and the ASMC?"

"Of course not. That's up to you to do. That way I can claim no knowledge of the conversation."

"He is smart." That was Warner from the background.

"Of course I'm smart." Denis' tone was haughty, making Cherry laugh. "I caught the biker, didn't I?"

"God, Denis. You are—" Cherry looked at his reflection again. "I'm so glad we met."

"Me, too, Tattoo. Me, too."

***

Denis

Home, and in his favorite lounge pants, Denis threw himself on the couch. He buried his face in the cushion and came up smiling. Just a hint of masculine scent, and it brought back all the memories of him and Cherry making out.

He'd only been home a half an hour and already missed Cherry like crazy.

"It's too early to ask him to move in."

Rolling his neck, he stared at the ceiling.

"No, for real. It's too early to ask him to move in with me. We're not at the 'rent a trailer to move him in' stage yet."

He sighed and rose from the couch, headed to the kitchen and the wine he had chilling in the refrigerator. Glass in hand, he returned to the couch, this time seating himself with more decorum as he grabbed the TV remote with his free hand.

Five minutes later the wine was gone and he still hadn't settled on a single thing to watch.

"Doom scrolling on the TV is a new low."

After speaking with Cherry earlier today, he'd halfway expected a visit so they could go over anything Ricky had found. Denis found himself resenting Cherry's absence far more than a 'not at the move in stage yet' should demand.

His phone buzzed and he nearly took a header off the couch leaning over to pluck it from the side table.

I should be home in about an hour. See you then.

At first, he was disappointed that Cherry was going home instead of coming here, then he read the text again, more slowly, and sat upright on the couch.

"He called my house home. This is home to him."

Maybe they were about to rent a trailer after all.

Chapter Twenty-One
Cherry

He went looking for Ruger or Busk, finding both men seated on facing chairs along one side of the room. Cherry grabbed another chair and pulled up to form the third leg of their triangle.

"I have something I want to run by you. We don't need privacy, I trust every man under the IMC patch." Cherry paused and waited for Ruger's approval. After he got the nod, he pulled in a breath. "This is all very coincidental, but I'm thinking there's a link. The other night when we hit ASMC, one of the prospects hanging around the burn barrel at the entrance looked familiar. I thought he did, anyway, but couldn't get the best look. You know how the ASMC prospects have their initials on their left shoulder?" Both men nodded, Busk looking at him with obvious impatience. "Hang on, Busk. Let me get to the good parts." That pulled a chuckle from Ruger.

"This prospect's initials were HL. I pulled a blank on anyone I knew with those initials, so I didn't spend much time puzzling at it. But today, in court, Warner said the rookie wasn't available because he got burned." He looked between the two men before dropping the bomb. "Rookie's name is Herbert LaBlanc. HL. I think that's too tight a spiral to be random."

"ASMC prospect-patched a fucking LEO? That's some fucking balls on the part of the prospect. Can you imagine if we did that? We'd be run out of town on the back of a lame cow."

Cherry stared at Busk for a minute, then shook his head.

"Yeah, sometimes I don't know where my mouth is going until we get there. But you get the gist. That's a hell of a mistake."

"What if it wasn't a mistake?" Ruger shook his head. "We've been surprised by how quickly this chapter of the ASMC has grown. They've got what? Seven prospects right now? Seven prospects to about twenty members. That's not a lotta mentorship time for any one member. Does this prospect LaBlanc have any other ties, outside of Warner?"

"I don't know, but I'll get Ricky working on it. He's going to be pissed he missed the connection."

"Probably make him work twice as hard." Cherry pushed to his feet. "Nice to see Daddy and Daddy made up and aren't fighting any longer."

"Oh, fuck you. Go get your guy already. Call Ricky in the morning."

"Won't have to twist my arm twice."

He pushed the door open and stepped into the quiet outside. He thumbed a message to Denis, trying to not rethink what he was admitting, even in small portions.

Coming home to you, baby.

***

He heaved out a sigh as he parked the bike on the street. He hated having it vulnerable to either a drive-by crash or four strong men in a van on a stealing spree.

"Wonder if there's protected parking close. I'll ask Denis. Be worth a monthly rental to have peace of mind."

Denis met him at the door with a kiss and a cold beer, and Cherry backed him into the kitchen with a steaming hot kiss. He put the beer on the counter and wrapped both his arms around Denis. "God I'm glad to be home. There's so much shit right now, you're like the center of a storm, I always feel just a bit calmer when I'm around you."

"I'm your whirling eye? That doesn't sound peaceful." Denis tilted Cherry's chin so he could attack the edge of his jaw. Cherry let his eyes drift closed, riding the wave of attraction and excitement.

"Did you know that makes me crazy?" He groaned softly. "Like legit crazy. Makes me want to tear your clothes off."

"Good to know," Denis said, lips moving against Cherry's skin.

At that moment, Cherry's phone buzzed from his front pocket.

"Ugh," he groaned. "What do they want now?" He pulled it from his pocket and answered it, just as Denis found another sensitive place, right behind the hinge of his jaw. "Legit crazy." He wasn't aware he'd whispered the word aloud until Busk started laughing. "What do you want?"

"Well, when I called it was to tell you we're starting back up about noon tomorrow. Still have a lot to hash out. But now, I want to know exactly what your Guy is doing that's making you, and I quote, 'Legit crazy'?"

"Fuck you. I'll be there by noon." He disconnected the call and tossed the phone on the counter. "Sorry, babe." Tipping his chin up, he stared into Denis' eyes. "I'm all yours now, at least until noon."

Denis arched one eyebrow and grinned. "Good to know. Grab your beer and let's head over to the makeout couch."

Cherry picked up the beer and took a deep drink. "The couch has a name now?"

"Of course. We have to accurately describe its new duties."

"'Of course,' he says, like that makes sense." Cherry followed Denis to the couch and sat on the end that had somehow become his, beer on the coaster on the table. He held out his arms and Denis came to him, settling on the cushions between Cherry's wide-spread legs. "Now, more about this couch."

"Sometimes a demonstration is the easiest way to understanding."

It was a couple hours later that they were moving to the bedroom and Cherry started chuckling as he walked through the door, Denis' hand in his. "Is this now the fucking bed? Because I could make an argument to that effect."

"And this solicitor wouldn't argue against."

***

Denis

He knew it was late, the darkness pressing against the windows. Denis had tried to keep from watching the clock, because not only would that not make time move faster, but it actually seemed to slow it considerably.

The light tap at the door sounded like a gunshot to the nervous Denis, and he snapped, "Come in already." *Maybe it's Cherry.*

Carole popped around the edge of the door. "Are you going to take my head off if I bother you?"

"No, of course not. I'm just on edge tonight. I don't know why."

"Lie number one. Even I know why, Denis." She shook her head and Denis noticed not one strand of hair moved.

"How do you do that?"

"Do what?"

"Do that thing with your hair."

"What thing with my hair?"

"That non-moving thing. I just realized I've never seen your hair move. Not even during Katrina. I clearly remember being able to use your hair as a boat. Never even took on water."

"Nephew, you are about to be on my last nerve. Hair spray, you might have heard of it? I remember you liking that musical, the one all about hair."

"The musical *Hair*?"

"That's what I just said." She threw up her hands and made to turn around.

"No, stay. I'm sorry. I'm just...I thought I'd have heard from Cherry before now."

Her chin lifted, expression sharpening. "What's he doing that's put him in danger's path?"

"What? I didn't say anything like that."

"Evidence exhibit one, you're still here at eleven o'clock at night. Lately if you're here until five it's rare. Which is a good thing and I'm not complaining. Better work and life balance is good for everyone." She tilted her head to the side. "Exhibit two, you're seriously on edge. You forget I can see your reflection in the windows. I was watching you for five minutes before I announced myself. You spent the entire time looking at your cell. Exhibit three, you haven't said you'll call him, but that you should have heard from him by now. Ergo, he's put himself in harm's way for some reason. Probably club business, and don't I know better than to ask after that."

"You are incorrigible."

"I'm incredibly flexible. Just ask Jinx."

Denis stared in horror at his aunt, his office manager, the woman who'd been mothering him for decades. "I do not want to know. Nope. I don't. Don't tell me."

"Jinx—"

"Nope," he interrupted whatever she'd been about to tell him. "Go home, Carole. Get some sleep for both of us. But for God's sake, I never want to know what happened between you and Jinx."

"What about Doodle? Did you know he's a legit artist? He's got two paintings in a local show right now."

"How do you find out about all of this?"

"I listen, child. Something I'd encourage you to do." She nodded at his hands and he realized his phone was ringing. "Tell him you love him already. I'll see myself out." The door closed behind her as he connected the call.

"Hey." Denis rolled his eyes at how lame that was. *It's Carole's fault, dropping that little bomb without warning.* "All well?"

"Now it is." Cherry pulled in a heavy breath. "I called, I mean I wanted to call and let you know I'm probably not going to make it home tonight. We're in the midst of a meeting that looks to be going on for a ridiculous amount of time. We broke for a few minutes so everyone could call their significant others." Heaving out a huge sigh, Cherry said, "I'll see you tomorrow, babe."

"Yes, tomorrow. Keep yourself safe for me."

"Will do. Yeah, I'm coming." That last was louder and carried a tone of irritation. "See you tomorrow." That last was said in a soft whisper.

The call disconnected and Denis was frozen in place staring at the phone in his hands.

"I'm his significant other."

***

Cherry

"Busk," Cherry called out as they headed back into the meeting room, air still thick with smoke. "Brother, why is Mother against us

220

hitting them again? I thought Wildman was all for it."

"Not sure, but this next portion is gonna be restricted to officers only. Members will be asked to hang in the main room. Hopefully Mother is a little bit more open." Busk pulled a palm over his face, scrubbing at his five o'clock shadow. "Junebug isn't happy about being home alone with the kiddos."

"Your kids are six or seven now, right?"

"Yeah, Todd is nearly eight and Landry is six. Then there's Willy, he's five. So she's got her hands full."

"Willy? You mean Ruger's boy? Or are you guys fostering or something?"

Busk froze in place, his eyes darting from Cherry to something behind him. Cherry turned to see Ruger on his way towards them, his expression matching Busk's.

"I...uh..." Busk couldn't get a word out.

"What's going on?" Ruger asked as he closed the distance with long strides.

"I...well...there's this—"

"Willy is my and Junebug's boy."

"Oh. Well. That's…" Cherry thought back to all the little clues he'd witnessed in the past six months. *A poly relationship.* "That actually makes sense. So, congrats. Five years late. Y'all all together?" He shook his head. "Ignore me, that's not my business, but—"

"And we'll keep it not your business," Busk found his voice. "But I'll tell you that Po'Boy and Wrench don't have a lock on kinky."

"Jesus, Busk. Thanks, Cherry. Let's get back on track," Ruger pointed towards the door to the back room. "I want a plan ironed out before we scatter."

"You and me both, brother." Cherry noticed Busk's gaze was fixed on Ruger, who appeared to be staring back. "So I'll just go back in. Y'all take your time."

None of my business what they do, long as it doesn't harm the club.

In the back room, Cherry regained his seat and looked around. Wildman had stayed in the room, so was in the lead position at the table.

Cherry narrowed his eyes. "We have to hit them."

"I know."

"If you know, then why are you blocking us?" Cherry was overwhelmed with anger. "If you know, let us do what's best for our chapter. I know that anything an individual chapter does can rebound back up to national, but this bullshit cannot stand."

"I know."

"Then what the actual fuck are we doing here? It feels like we're arguing about pennies when the Benjamins are slipping out the door. What do you need from us to move past whatever the blockage is?"

Wildman leaned closer, then shouted, "We're waiting on the right time."

"You fucker," Cherry jerked back from where he'd been leaning into Wildman. "What does Mother believe is the right time?"

"You know Myron, the Rebel Wayfarers' lead IT guy?" Wildman caught Cherry's gaze with his own. "I'm waiting to hear from him. He believed he had a way to make this easier. I trust

Myron, he wouldn't have asked for time if he didn't have a good solution."

"Jesus, Wildman. All you had to do was say that. Everyone here holds the Rebels in high regard. But you're IMC, man, shouldn't you have talked to our lead IT guy before handing the keys over to a different club?"

"I would have, but Pony was already on the call with Myron. They're working on it together. That good enough for you?" Wildman lifted one eyebrow, then broke the serious moment with a grin.

"I'm just gonna sit here and wait, then." Cherry slouched as he glared at Wildman. "Wanna run a plan through on how we deal with LaBlanc? A mind exercise."

"Sure. Are we certain he's playing all sides of the dice? Rookie cop, Prospect in ASMC, corrupt as hell and pulling arrests based on informant info?"

"That last has stopped now, because he doesn't have an informant anymore." Busk pulled out a chair and plopped down.

"Right, but he's still a cop and a prospect in an outlaw club. Those two things shouldn't exist." Ruger slipped into the seat between Cherry and Busk, as if they were facing Wildman down.

"Y'all are intimidating as hell." Wildman laughed and pointed a finger at each of them in turn. "But I am not intimidated. I'm impressed, which is different."

The phone on the table in front of Wildman buzzed and he answered it immediately. After a moment, he switched gears and put the device on the table between them, turning on the speaker.

"Say all that again, Myron."

"We found the link. It's LaBlanc. He's got a lotta money in an offshore, looks like he's been skimming from a few places, one of them the club he's trying to patch into. It looks like ASMC head honchos are starting to get nervous, and he's the one they're investigating—"

"You have all the documentation, right? You can send that here?" Cherry broke in with his question.

"Hell yeah we've got the docs." That was Pony. "Shut up and listen, Cherry."

"As ordered." Cherry sat back in his chair.

"We've got two different paths we can take. One would be an anonymous tip to the cops, and let their IA folks deal with him. Odds that he'd lose his job are high. Odds that he'd pay for his bullshit, low to medium."

"And the second route?" Wildman leaned closer to the phone. "I'm not liking the outcome of the first option."

"We do a meet with ASMC heads. They do have a mother chapter, it's just not billed as such. The chapter in Jacksonville is where they started."

"Jacksonville, Texas? We need to get in touch with Blackie's folks?"

"Nope, because that might make sense. Jacksonville, Florida. They have exactly two chapters, mother and Baton Rouge." Myron's voice communicated his level of disbelief. "Fucking six hundred miles between their only two groups. That's just asking for a mess."

"Where does this meet happen?" Cherry was already running various scenarios in his head.

"Right where you are, and in about thirty minutes. They're already on a plane headed your way and should be landing at Metro in less than five."

Silence descended on the men around the table, each of them showing some level of astonishment. Cherry finally broke the quiet and asked, "Say what? Say again? I don't think I caught that."

"Yes you did, Cherry." Pony cut in, his voice trembling with glee. "Thirty minutes to get the hangarounds driven off, get the main room set for a meeting, and explain to the members they'll stand around the edge and won't interrupt. Get busy, big man. Chop, chop."

"Jesus wept." Cherry pushed back from the table. "Hope they're not expecting any pleasantries because we're going to just jump off the dock into the deep end. Are you already sending the documentation to me?"

"You and the other three men sitting with you."

"Good job, I gotta go get shit sorted." He paused. "Good job, Pony, Myron. Thanks for your work. Also, good to meet you, Myron. Heard a lot of good things about you. Sure you don't want to patch over to IMC?"

"No, he does not." A deep voice echoed over the phone's speaker, and Wildman nearly fell out of his chair laughing. "This is Mason, and Myron is mine."

A click indicated the call had ended and Cherry looked around the room at the men, all laughing. "Was it something I said?" He rolled his eyes and moved to the front room. This was where they'd meet, not in the room the chapter used for church. He got the furniture movement lined out, and turned to the bar with a set of instructions. Hangarounds got the eviction notice, and prospects understood they were parking lot security, nothing more. Cherry toggled to the app the club used for communication and keyed up an all-hands message. If they could get to the clubhouse within twenty minutes, they were to come. If not, stay away. He didn't want any members coming in after they were seated.

Finally, he took a minute to review the information forwarded to his phone via the secure app. Each was more damning than the previous. LaBlanc had been playing all aspects of his life off each other.

Wildman strolled up next to him. "Pretty cut and dried."

"I want him here for it. That would be ideal. But we've got—" He checked his watch. "—less than twenty minutes now."

"Lemme see what I can do." Wildman pulled out his phone and stepped outside, already talking before the door closed. "Myron, one more thing—"

"Ruger, Busk, wanna chat a minute." Cherry tilted his head towards the door leading to the back room. The two men followed him and Busk closed the door.

He started talking as soon as the door clicked shut. "Here's what I know. Atlas is their president, Loki the VP, and don't you wonder how he got that name? Anyway, Enforcer is also coming, and he's Simba. ASMC has been based out of Jacksonville for years, it's a generational club. One member's kid took off and that's where we get the Baton Rouge chapter. That's Apollo. His old man was a lifer, just like Atlas' old man, and so on. In Jacksonville, they are a white knight club, and nothing Myron or Pony can dig up says that they knew about what's been going on here. This might be a quick meeting."

Ruger nodded. "Or it might be a longer, more important meeting. I've got Twisted on speed dial, just in case there's anything significant to discuss."

***

"Naw, man. We've got nothing to discuss." Atlas shook his head for about the fifteenth time. "We're not moving dope through your territory. My guys assured me they're staying on the Texas side of the line for any off-book runs." He pointed over to where LaBlanc was seated along the wall, held in the chair by the heavy hands of two IMC members pressing down on his shoulders. "I don't know what to say about that one. His probation wasn't run past our Jacksonville guys. I'll have to get with the others. Or, know what? I'd very much like to have Apollo and Dillinger here. I understand wanting to take the trash to the top tier, but I'd like to hear what they have to say before we go any further."

Cherry grit his teeth until his jaw hurt. These assholes weren't understanding what was going on right under their nose. They'd perked up at the four million LaBlanc had stashed offshore, but other than that they'd waved off anything the IMC officers had laid out. He didn't know where Wildman was finding the patience to deal, because he'd have thrown a table by now.

"Then let's get them here." Wildman pulled out his phone and dialed. "Hey Apollo, this is Wildman. Would you mind a quick trip to the IMC clubhouse here in Baton Rouge? Bring Dilly if you would. No, not much, just something to discuss." He paused, tilting his head up as he listened. "Yeah, I'm still hopeful we can work something out. That's why I wanna talk to you tonight." Another pause, then he grinned, the expression feral and vicious. "See you in ten." Leaning back in his chair, he tossed the phone to the tabletop. "On their way, Atlas." He sat up suddenly. "Say, does your club have something about Greek mythology? I just realized you've got Atlas and Apollo, but then Loki is Norse. And

Simba and Dillinger don't fit the schema. Is there a schema?"

"Oh, hell no. Don't get him started." Loki laughed as he spoke up for the first time during the meeting. "He can go on and on about Greek versus Norse, or Hindu lined up against Egyptian. Everything is a mythology, if it's old enough and someone wrote a book about it."

Atlas grinned good naturedly. "I'm not that bad."

"You are exactly that bad, brother." Loki leaned against the table. "Last year we were down at Daytona and he about got in a fight with a Rebels' guy. The shouting match was like flame to tinder."

"Who was it?" Wildman asked intently.

"Bones. He debated well. We were having a good time before someone broke it up." Atlas pretended to glower at Loki.

"Yeah, Bones is a good one. We're allied with the Rebels here, and all along the coast. It pays to have good relationships with other clubs." Wildman tipped his head up. "They should be rolling in any minute." A heavy sigh was followed by a low hum. "If they're going to show, that is."

"Why wouldn't they show?" Atlas seemed genuinely taken aback. "If they said they'd be here, why wouldn't they show?"

"Let's say they know what LaBlanc is doing, condoned it, and maybe even organized it. That'd be one reason to not show." Wildman yawned, appearing totally at ease. "Let's say they're spending their minutes looking for LaBlanc over there. Looking but not finding. Let's say they have an inkling the job has gone sideways. They wouldn't be within fifty miles of this clubhouse." He lifted his head and looked over at Cherry. "Brother, which way are you betting?"

"Hundred says they don't show. But I'd be taking your money while knowing the future." He pulled out his phone and unlocked it. "Let me see here. If I do this—" He tapped the screen. "—and then do that. Well, lookie here. They are headed up north somewhere. Looks like they got on the interstate and are just rolling away." He held up the phone so the two ASMC officers could see the map with its cluster of dots. Two were red and leading the cluster. "Those red dots are Apollo and Dillinger. The rest are a slice of the members. There's not enough of them on the road, so let's scroll down. Oh, yep, the rest are at the clubhouse. Which is interesting. Why wouldn't the whole club roll out for a run?"

"You bugged our club?" Loki looked dangerous when he was that alert. "You bugged our members?"

"Not all of them." Cherry shook his head. "But the two leaders and a few of their closest confidants? Hell yeah." He stood, leaning over the table. "Because this isn't a fucking game. It's not a week at Daytona, cruising the line. This is fucking life and death around here, and they're trying to shit on what we've built. I will not allow it. Nope, that I will not allow."

"Do you know where they're going?" Atlas pushed his chair back. "I'm in favor of going to talk to the members left in town."

"Oh, you do that. LaBlanc here can ride with us. I have a good idea where they're headed. There's a couple of RCs up north, just east of the interstate. Rumor was they were friendly with your Scimitars. I'd be looking for a bolt hole if I were them, and those RC could provide it." Cherry stood and crowded close to

Atlas and Loki. "Your invitation is revoked. You'll need to be on the plane to get a ride home." He looked over his shoulder. "Busk, what time is that plane leaving?"

"Six o'clock on the dot. Don't be late." Busk stood and stepped up so he was shoulder to shoulder with Cherry. Ruger moved into place on his other side.

Cherry watched as Atlas swallowed hard. "We won't be late. I'm going to go see if I can salvage the members who didn't cut and run. Would you let me know what you find when you catch up to Apollo?" Atlas stuck out his hand.

"Prolly. Depending on what we find. Some messages are better delivered in person." Ruger didn't move from his position and Atlas' hand hung there for another beat before he pulled back, standing tall again. "Don't call me, I'll call you."

Cherry watched them exit the building, Loki taking his place at his President's six. "They've got balls."

The door closed behind them and Cherry heard a cage engine start outside.

"They do, or they didn't know what they were walking into. I don't know if I'd have had the gonads to stand up to a rival club's president, knowing it was just me and Busk. I believe I would, but it would have been a pucker moment. Kudos to them." Ruger turned to face Cherry. "I want you already gone."

"Yup." Cherry pointed at a dozen men in turn. "You're coming with me." He pointed at another six men. "You're coming with me as well, but when we're closer in we'll push you to roll in five minutes behind us. Hopefully we won't need the help, but I'd rather be safe than sorry."

Jinx, one of the men selected for the delayed entry, grinned. "Just call us the Savin' Bacon crew."

Busk leaned closer. "How are you dealing with LaBlanc?"

"Easy as," Cherry said, walking over to where the man still sat. He reached to his back, pulling out his gun. The Glock fit his hand, settling into place immediately. He pulled back, noted LaBlanc's delayed reaction, and clocked him on the side of his head. The man immediately went boneless, slipping from the chair into a pile on the floor. "That should keep him for as long as we need. Someone get zip ties on his wrists and ankles. Put him in the room out back. He can wait for me there."

"Thought you were taking him?" Salty hefted LaBlanc to his shoulder in a fireman's carry.

"Not a fucking chance. Can you imagine having him laid across the seat and running past the po-lice?" He shook his head. "Not a fucking chance."

"Was afraid you'd lost what's left of your mind." Salty grinned. "Let me deposit this asshole in the room. Don't leave without me!"

"Wouldn't dream." Cherry offered his hand to Ruger and got pulled into a one-armed clinch. "I'm not planning on bringing anyone back, brother."

"Just ours. Fuck the assholes."

Busk pulled on Cherry's arm, spinning him into a one-armed hug. "Call your guy before you go."

Cherry paused. He'd been so focused on business, it hadn't crossed his mind. "Will do."

He raised his voice. "My guys, we go in five. Roll heavy, bring sparklers." Cherry watched as each man checked for his weapon of choice, and then pulled lengths of chain from the closet near the door. He turned back to the meeting room, pulling his phone out.

Got a minute for a quick call?

The answer came almost immediately as his phone rang in his hand.

"Hey. I was just thinking of you."

Cherry felt a grin lift the corners of his mouth. "Oh yeah? What were you thinking?"

"Not sure it's proper for mixed company."

"Ah, you've got visitors. I'll keep it brief. We're headed out to deal with the ASMC in a final way. I should be home, but it'll be late."

"Home." Denis spoke softly and Cherry matched his tone.

"Yeah, home." He paused, more words dancing on the tip of his tongue, but he bit them back. "See you soon." It physically hurt to press the button to disconnect the call.

I should have told him.

There'll be time.

***

Cherry lifted his fist, signaling for the column to pull to the side of the road. It had been ten minutes since they'd passed the last car, something Cherry found encouraging. He slowed to a halt, standing with the still-running bike between his legs. Pulling out his phone, he saw a call request waiting, and connected, twisting to look up into the sky.

"I see you but you can't see me." Pony's laughter was loud. "I'm loving these new drones. The Rebels get the coolest toys."

"How close are we? Within five miles?"

"Three point two. Good guestimate."

"Detour in place? I shouldn't even ask. Of course it is."

Pony laughed again. "As planned, bossman. You want the rundown now?"

"Yes, please." Cherry listened intently.

"Eight ASMC. That's all that have stayed with Apollo and Dillinger. No old ladies, no kiddos."

"Just assholes." Cherry sighed. "Next you'll tell me they're drunk off their asses."

"Nope. They even have two sentinels on the road headed into the clubhouse. Just as you turn on, and a half mile past."

"Noted. Hey, do you have lethal action on that fancy drone?"

"Let me check into that, won't take a minute." He heard a keyboard tapping, and then Pony made a pleased sound. "Incapacitating action. Deployed now, and will do again before you get there if needed. I'll park the drones above the individual locations."

"Fuckin' rad, brother. Have you been able to see the RC folks?"

Pony paused, voice coming out in a deep rasp. "Dead from what I can see on the drone video. I'm guessing they didn't appreciate the invasion."

"Fuck."

"Exactly."

"Okay, do you have an estimate for the assholes' guns?"

"Normal individual pieces, but the RC liked to do boomies, so there's a fuckton of Tannerite. It's just laying around on tables and shit."

"Well, that is inconvenient. No random shots, got it."

"Busk wants a call."

"'Dokies. Text me if there's anything I need to know."

"Yup. Shiny side up, brother."

"You know it, Pony. Later, brother."

Before he could do more than pull the phone away from his ear it was ringing. Busk.

"Brother?" Cherry didn't elaborate on the greeting. He didn't need to.

"Cherry, I just got off the phone with Twisted. He and Atlas came to an agreement. They will patch over. The Jacksonville club will be easy, straight patch ceremony. All the members are in agreement."

"Sounds like a good solution. Absorb before we have problems." Cherry's mind raced ahead. "What about the ones I'm chasing?"

"They've been removed from the member roster. Atlas informed each of the men what the outcome would be if they didn't immediately return to the clubhouse. That handful of men are who refused. They're no longer in a club, rival or not."

"So now they are individual assholes who need to answer for their sins. Got it. Can you tell Pony to expect a cleaner call in a few?"

"Will do."

"And what's happening with the rest of the ASMC there in Baton Rouge?"

"They're going to need a good Enforcer lesson or two."

"Of course they are. Maybe I can find a good apprentice in the ranks soon."

"If it's a heavy burden, brother, we should talk."

"I found my guy, man."

"I'll let Ruger know we need to have a confab."

"Okay, I'm going to go deal with these assholes."

He hung up as he twisted and pointed to Jinx. "Hey, Savin' Bacon, there are two drones ahead that are parked over the top of two men you need to bring in. Don't care how you do it, long as it gets done."

"Understood." Jinx pointed to two of the men in his crew and they had a quiet conversation while Cherry glanced at the other men.

"There's Tannerite laying around inside the clubhouse. That kinda precludes going in guns blazing. Use chains if you think you're controlled enough, otherwise it's going to be an old fashioned knuckle sandwich beatdown. Anyone have questions?"

No one raised a hand, and he nodded. "Let's roll."

***

Cherry stood with his back to the clubhouse wall, listening to the conversations going on inside.

"Those IMC pussies aren't going to do anything. We'll own Red Stick before you know it."

"ASMC in charge. Changes are going to be happening, brothers. We'll lay down the law to everyone on two wheels."

He couldn't identify the two speakers. Probably Apollo and Dillinger, but it didn't really matter, they were openly discussing attacking his club, his brothers. *Make bad choices, get shitty prizes.*

He pointed at the front door, then at Salty and Jinx. A finger pointed at himself, and the rest of the club were directed around the corner to where the back door was. Both were open, pulling fresh air through the club. *Typical bayou life.*

The sound of movement came from inside the clubhouse. Cherry lifted a fist and looked around, then pumped it twice. They were inside in moments. The chaos was divided between the doors, as expected. He saw Salty throw two punches and take down his man. A man with terror on his face approached and Cherry cocked one arm back, meeting the man's momentum with his own. He went down like a broken marionette.

Another man tried to run past, and Cherry grabbed his arm, swinging him in a half circle. Doodle was there with a hammer blow, and another ASMC reject hit the dirt.

Silence fell around him, and he looked back and forth. "Not a single shot fired. Love it." Two IMC men had taken a knee, and he pointed towards them. "Get some aid going." Doodle nodded and moved towards the two men, but then paused.

"Uh, Enforcer? I'm thinking you need some, too." Face bloody from a split lip, Salty appeared in front of Cherry and steered him back against the wall.

Cherry pushed against the hold. "Get off, brother. I've got to deal with final arrangements."

"You're bleeding, Enforcer. Let's give it a gander. Long as you're not spurting, I'll back off."

Cherry held the edges of his vest out wide, letting Salty have access to whatever he'd seen.

"Survivors need to be restrained and taken outside." He motioned to the two members riding herd on the failed lookouts. "Take them out back, too."

"You'll survive." Salty backed up. "I'd like to get it packed, but that can wait. You're not quite bleeding like a stuck pig. I don't like it, but you should go and carry out the judgement."

"Got it." Cherry looked around the room, surprised to find three men still on the floor. The two he'd interacted with and another by the front door. "These three toes up?"

"Yup. You're a hella deadly Enforcer, I like it." Salty grinned, then licked at his split lip, more blood trickling down his chin. "Fuckin' glad you're on our team, brother."

"Three down. Three to go." Cherry clenched and released his fist a few times, finally feeling the sting of busted knuckles and aching flesh. "I'm glad we're on the same team, too, man."

Outside there were three men in a line kneeling in the dirt, bound hands lifted behind their backs, forcing their heads down.

"Which ones are Apollo and Dillinger?" He saw a prisoner jerk at the question and pointed at him. "Which one is he?"

"Dillinger, the VP. Apollo is still inside."

"Not no more he isn't. Get those colors off them. ASMC is no more, we're going to burn all those vests." He watched as men went to work on removing the vests.

A man shouted in pain and Cherry saw Jinx shrug. "Oops."

"Listen—" Cherry turned when the door opened behind him. Several bodies were being carried outside, these were the RC members that ASMC had slaughtered. "Know what? Never mind." He walked behind the first man, pulled his gun, and in a smooth movement slotted the muzzle against the back of the man's head. "Goodbye." He squeezed the trigger, then took two steps to put himself behind the next man. And then the next.

Cherry winced; the kickback of the gun had set his side on fire.

"Hey, Salty," Jinx called, "Enforcer needs a little more TLC."

"On it." Salty was in Cherry's face, then an arm slipped underneath his own, holding him up. "Let's go back inside so I can get at things better. Hey, Sir, can you grab that bag off my bike again?" He must have received an affirmative response because Salty grunted out, "Thanks."

"Report on our injured?"

"Other than you, you mean?"

"Don't crawl up my ass, Salty. Just give me a rundown."

"One with bruised, or more likely, broken ribs. We'll dope him and he can ride his bike back, no problem. Second with a through-and-through in his leg. No major structures compromised, but he's got a fucking big hole in his skin. I've got him packed and wrapped, and he should be good to go, it's not his shifter leg." Salty maneuvered Cherry to a chair and pushed him into it. "Do you know who did the stabby stabby to you?"

"Is that what it is?" Cherry looked down and noticed a hole in his vest. "Fucking asshole pegged my cut."

"We'll stitch around it in celebration of your survival." Salty took a pack from Sir Loin, then gestured at Cherry. "Hold his arms up, yeah?"

Fingers probed where the fire was worst, where the small blaze was burning, and with the attention it flared into a wildfire.

"The fuck. That hurts."

"Good, means you aren't in shock. Give me another thirty seconds and I'll start packing it. The blade nicked two ribs, the bones keeping the knife from slamming home. I just want to get the splinters out."

Another probe unleashed a new wave of fire that had Cherry gritting his teeth together hard.

"Nearly done, brother?" The pressure disappeared and Cherry pulled in a breath. He looked down for the first time, noticing the swath of blood that went from his sternum to the hem of his shirt. Lifting the tail, he saw a hole with a plug of what looked like fabric. "This gonna hold until tomorrow?"

"Should, long as you don't engage in too vigorous activity." Salty was grinning, brows waggling suggestively. "You know what I mean."

Cherry pulled out his phone and made the necessary calls, beginning with one to Wildman about the cache of Tannerite they'd danced around tonight. His next call started a cleaning crew moving towards the RC clubhouse. He counted seventeen dead. *All of them because of ASMC's useless fucking decisions. Instead of standing and taking their medicine, they had to come up here and ruin more lives.*

Ignoring the anger still circling through his gut, he sent one final text, *Done. Coming home to you.*

Chapter Twenty-Two
Denis

He stared at his phone, willing it to ring. Or buzz. Or anything but the dead silence for the past several hours.

As if called by his stubborn gaze, the device buzzed. Just once. But when Denis picked up the phone and read it, the message carried much more than just information.

Done. Coming home to you.

"Coming home to me. I'm his home." Weight he hadn't realized he was carrying lifted from his shoulders.

Earlier tonight he'd been out for a post-work nightcap with Carole, and the moment the call with Cherry had disconnected he'd regretted not making that conversation a priority. "Won't make that mistake again. I'll be taking all his calls. Gonna make sure he knows it, too."

Quickly he thumbed a response, wincing when it stuck on Delivering for several seconds. Finally, the little flag changed, to not just Sent, but Read.

I'll be waiting.

He stared at the phone for a few minutes, willing it to buzz again, or ring, or anything else. Finally he shoved it in the pocket of his slacks.

"Okay," he addressed the empty room. "What will he need when he gets home. A shower, he likes to shower after a long ride. He'll probably be hungry." He nodded. "That's the plan. Start a pan of something, and set the shower up. Good plan." He clapped once. "Break. Go team."

In the kitchen, he did what his father had always done when stuck for a meal. Into one pot went spices, potatoes, tomatoes, cut up sausage, and canned chicken broth. "That's started, it can simmer until he gets home." He prepared a bowl of rice and ran cool water over it. Swishing his fingers through the water, he stirred it gently, watching as the water changed color. Straining the washed rice, he put it in a pot with a lid and set it aside. "That can wait. I'll be back." Denis shook his head. "Who are you talking to, fool?"

The bathroom attached to the main bedroom was big, with a walk-in shower featuring multiple waterheads. Cherry had mentioned more than once how nice it was. Hot water on demand, massage heads, towel warmer. Oh yeah, Denis had gone all out when he'd done a remodel several years ago. Now, every time he shared the shower with Cherry, he'd thanked his past self.

He turned on the towel warmer and draped a couple of towels over the bars. Inside the shower, he put a new bottle of bodywash, the spicy scent he had noticed Cherry liked. Denis went back into the bedroom and grabbed a robe, hanging it on a peg next to the shower.

Returning to the kitchen, Denis stirred the makeshift jambalaya and tasted it. "More salt," he mused, grabbing the shaker and giving it a good rattle. Stirring again, he tasted again. "Just about right."

He left it to simmer and went to the living room, turning on the TV. He watched the news with some anxiety, as if whatever job

Cherry had been working on today would wind up on the evening news.

Denis woke several hours later when the door rattled open. He pushed up from the couch and met Cherry as he came through the entryway, the door shutting behind him.

Denis held Cherry close, the biker's leather vest creaking under his grip, the faint scent of smoke and sweat clinging to him like a shadow. Cherry's arms tightened around Denis's waist, but there was a hitch in his breath, a subtle wince that made Denis pull back just enough to scan his face. Under the hallway light, Cherry looked worn, his storm-gray eyes shadowed with exhaustion, a split knuckle on one hand, and a dark stain blooming through the side of his shirt beneath the vest.

"You're hurt," Denis murmured, his voice thick with concern. He cupped Cherry's jaw, thumb brushing over the stubble, feeling the tension there. "Come on, let's get you cleaned up."

Cherry nodded, his usual gruff smirk softened by fatigue. "Just a scratch, Suit Guy. Nothin' I can't handle."

But he let Denis lead him, first to the kitchen to turn off the stove, and then with one arm slung over Denis's shoulder they made their way to the bedroom. The air was warm, the faint hum of the towel warmer a comforting backdrop. Denis eased Cherry down onto the edge of the bed, taking his vest with reverence, folding it and placing it on top of the nearby dresser. He then knelt in front of Cherry to tug off his boots first, the heavy thuds echoing in the quiet room. Cherry watched him, eyes hooded, something vulnerable flickering in their depths.

"Shirt off," Denis said softly, his hands gentle as he helped peel the blood-stiffened fabric away. He sucked in a breath at the sight; there was a jagged wound along Cherry's side, packed with gauze but seeping slightly, the skin around it bruised purple and raw. "Jesus, Cherry. This isn't a scratch."

Cherry's hand came up, covering Denis's where it hovered over the injury. "Knife glanced off my ribs. Salty patched me up good. It'll heal." His voice was low, rough, but there was a tremor in it, not from pain, but from the weight of the night. "Missed you, Denis. Thought about you the whole damn time."

Denis's chest ached, a swell of emotion rising like a tide. He leaned in, pressing a soft kiss to Cherry's collarbone, away from the bruises, tasting salt and skin. "I was scared," he admitted, voice barely above a whisper. "Waiting here, not knowing...I love you, Cherry. God, I love you so much it hurts."

Cherry froze for a heartbeat, then his fingers threaded into Denis's hair, pulling him up for a kiss that was slow and deep, like they were breathing each other in. "You're mine, lawyer man," Cherry rasped against his lips, his free hand clutching Denis's shirt. "Love you too. Been fightin' it, but...yeah. Love you."

The words hung between them, raw and real, and Denis felt tears prick his eyes. He kissed Cherry again, softer this time, mindful of the wounds, his hands mapping the familiar planes of Cherry's chest with care. He eased Cherry back onto the bed, propping pillows behind him to keep pressure off his side. "Let me take care of you," Denis whispered, grabbing a fresh towel from the warmer and the first-aid kit he'd stashed nearby.

Cherry's breath hitched as Denis gently peeled away the old gauze, cleaning the wound with antiseptic wipes, his touch feather-light. "Feels good," Cherry murmured, eyes locked on Denis's face, the vulnerability there stripping away the enforcer's armor. Denis applied fresh ointment, rebandaging it with steady hands, then kissed the edge of the dressing, trailing his lips up Cherry's ribs, over unmarred skin.

"You're beautiful," Denis said, voice breaking a little as he stripped off his own shirt, needing the closeness. He straddled Cherry carefully, thighs bracketing his hips without putting weight on the injured side. Their kisses deepened, slow and languid, tongues exploring with a tenderness that built like a quiet storm. Cherry's hands roamed Denis's back, calluses rough against smooth skin, pulling him closer.

Denis reached for the lube on the nightstand, warming it between his fingers before sliding a hand down, undoing Cherry's jeans with deliberate slowness. Cherry groaned softly, lifting his hips just enough, his hardness freed into Denis's palm. "Easy," Denis soothed, stroking him gently, watching Cherry's face for any sign of pain. "Tell me if it hurts."

"Only hurts when you're not touching me," Cherry replied, his voice gravelly with need.

He tugged at Denis's pants, helping shove them down, and soon they were skin to skin, bodies aligning in a careful rhythm. Denis prepared himself first, then Cherry, fingers gliding up and down with aching slowness, drawing out gasps and whispers of "please" from the biker beneath him.

When Denis finally sank down onto Cherry, it was inch by inch, gaze never leaving each other's. Cherry's hands gripped his hips, guiding but not rushing, their breaths syncing in the dim light. "Love you," Cherry whispered again, like a mantra, as Denis rocked slowly, the motion intimate, emotional, every thrust a confession. Tears slipped down Denis's cheeks, mingling with sweat, and Cherry thumbed them away, pulling him down for a kiss that tasted like salt and forever.

They moved together, unhurried, the build-up a sweet ache that crested in waves. It was Cherry's release spilling between them first, his body arching just enough to pull at the wound but not enough to stop. Denis followed, shuddering, collapsing carefully onto Cherry's good side, their limbs tangled.

In the quiet after, Denis traced patterns on Cherry's chest, listening to his heartbeat steady. "Stay with me," he murmured. "Always."

"Always," Cherry echoed, kissing his forehead. "Home's right here."

"Oh, we're seeing a doctor in the morning. If I'm keeping you, I'm keeping you healthy."

Cherry's laughter rattled Denis' head. But he simply said, "Betcha Jinx already called it in. Doc will probably be here by seven or so."

Chapter Twenty-Three

Cherry

The late afternoon sun dipped low over the Louisiana bayou, painting the sky in streaks of orange and purple as Cherry guided the motorcycle down the winding backroads towards the Incoherent MC clubhouse. The engine thrummed beneath them, a steady rumble that vibrated through his bones and soul. Heat grew from where Denis's chest pressed close behind him. Cherry's hands gripped the handlebars with easy confidence, but every now and then, he'd reach back with one gloved hand to squeeze Denis's thigh, a silent reminder that this—*them*—was real.

Weeks had passed since that blood-soaked night, the one where Cherry had come home to Denis battered and raw, whispering confessions in the dim light of their bedroom. Months of healing, not just the knife wound that had scarred his side but the deeper cuts to his soul, the ones he'd carried for decades.

The wind whipped past, and Cherry felt peace settle over him like the warm leather of his cut. The IMC had thrived in the aftermath. The ASMC's remnants had been absorbed or scattered, their colors burned in a bonfire that had lit up the night like a promise kept. LaBlanc had vanished into the night with Simba from Azrael's Scimitars stepping up and taking out the trash. For the men he'd been working with, they quickly found cops and feds closing in after documents Myron and Pony unearthed hit the right desks.

No loose ends, no blowback.

The chapter had grown stronger, tighter, with Busk and Ruger at the helm, and Cherry...Cherry had found his balance. The enforcer's role still called for iron fists when needed, but now it sat alongside something softer, something he'd never imagined in his whole life. Every wish had brought him closer to a life with Denis. Mornings tangled in sheets, evenings with takeout and case files scattered on the coffee table, nights where Cherry's rough edges met Denis's sharp wit and they melded into something unbreakable.

"Turn up here?" Denis shouted over the roar, his arms tightening around Cherry's waist as they approached the familiar gravel turnoff. His voice carried that easy laugh, the one that still made Cherry's pulse kick up like he was a prospect again.

"Yeah, babe," Cherry called back, downshifting as they eased onto the club lot. Bikes lined the edges like watchmen, glossy paint gleaming under strings of outdoor bulbs that flickered to life as dusk crept in. The clubhouse pulsed with life: laughter spilling from open doors, the sizzle of burgers on the grill, prospects hauling coolers of beer while old ladies and sweetbutts darted around with platters of ribs and cornbread. A party like this was like victory laps after a clean run, no cops on tails, no rivals sniffing at borders and it felt like breathing after years underwater.

Cherry killed the engine, the sudden quiet amplifying the bass thump of zydeco from the speakers. He swung off first, offering Denis a hand, pulling him close for a quick, possessive kiss that tasted like road dust and freedom.

Denis grinned down at him, hair tousled from the helmet, his button-down shirt untucked and casual.

Cherry had officially come out to the club months back, not long after what Busk and Ruger referred to as "the impound lot business." They'd all clapped him on the back, poured shots, and Busk had muttered something about "love finding a way" with a wink that hid the sap under his gruff exterior. The brothers? They rolled with it. Shades of gray in a world of black and white leather. Cherry was still the Enforcer, still the steady hand, but now he was whole. Everything in balance, his truth surviving the sun, and his heart happily claimed. No more hiding, no more shadows.

"Look at you two," Rook hollered from the porch, a beer in one hand and a cigar in the other. He lumbered over, pulling Cherry into a back-slapping hug that jostled the fresh tattoo peeking from under his sleeve, a small, discreet heart inked with "D" that matched the one Denis had surprised him with last week. "Brought the lawyer man to the den of wolves. Brave fucker."

Denis laughed, shaking Rook's hand with that firm, courtroom grip. "Wolves? Nah, this is my pack now. Wouldn't miss a party like this."

The night unfolded like a well-oiled ride: plates piled high with grilled meats and fixings, stories swapped around fire pits where the air crackled with heat and half-truths. Cherry kept Denis close, his arm slung over the back of a picnic bench, fingers tracing lazy circles on his shoulder. Diesel, arm healed and sling long gone, recounted the highway clip with exaggerated flair, drawing roars from the crowd, and sympathy from the pretty sweetbutt sitting on his lap. T-Bone passed around a bottle of bourbon, toasting to "the big dogs who keep the pack strong." And through it all, Cherry watched Denis, *his* Denis, charm the room, trading barbs with Busk about some pro bono case, laughing at Pony's tech jokes like he'd been patching in for years.

As the stars wheeled overhead, the bonfire roaring higher, Busk climbed onto a crate with a mic scavenged from god-knows-where, the feedback screeching before he tapped it quiet. The crowd hushed, bottles clinking to a stop. Busk's eyes, sharp under that perpetual scowl, found Cherry and Denis in the throng, a grin cracking his beard.

"Brothers, sisters, hangarounds, and...well, you know who you are," Busk started, voice booming with that VP gravel. Laughter rippled. "Tonight, we raise a glass to the IMC because we are stronger than ever, from Florida's Great Bend, to Hammond, and always to the Texas line. We've burned bridges, patched colors, and stared down the reaper. But more than that..." He paused, locking eyes with Cherry, then Denis. "We've got men like Cherry here, who enforces not just with fists, but with heart. And his man, Denis, who's got our backs in ways no gavel can touch. To loyalty, to love that don't bend. May it ride forever."

The cheers erupted, bottles and cans smashing together in a chaotic toast. Cherry's throat tightened, that old war drum in his chest now beating steady, not frantic. He pulled Denis against him, kissing him deep right there under the lights, the club's roar fading to a hum. "Told you they'd take to you," he murmured against Denis's lips.

Denis's eyes sparkled, hand fisting in Cherry's cut. "They're alright. But you're my ride, Tattoo. Always."

Cherry laughed, low and free, the weight of years lifting like smoke into the night. The club thrummed around them, this found family, forged in steel and fire, and here, with Denis by his side, Cherry was at peace. His truth was no longer buried, his love no longer a secret. Just a man on a bike, with his heart in the wind, riding towards whatever came next.

The End

ABOUT THE AUTHOR

Raised in the south, MariaLisa learned about the magic of books at an early age. Every summer, she would spend hours in the local library, devouring books of every genre. Self-described as a book-a-holic, she says "I've always loved to read, but then I discovered writing, and found I adored that, too. For reading...if nothing else is available, I've been known to read the back of the cereal box."

Also by MariaLisa deMora

Alace Sweets

A dark thriller, this book is not a light read. Filled with edge-of-your-seat suspense, this intense story commands the reader's attention as it drives towards the explosive ending. Alace Sweets is a vigilante serial killer, with everything that implies and is sure to trip all your triggers. Be ready.

At seventeen, Alace Sweets turned a corner in her life, taking the wrong shortcut home from school.

Resisting the harsh knowledge her attackers will never be made to pay for their actions, Alace takes a stand. Justice must be served, and if fate's scales are out of balance, she's determined to set things right as best she can.

When the laws of men fail, the rules of Alace prevail.

5-Star Reviews for Alace Sweets

"deMora has a superb story-line and exceptional character development. All of her characters have such depth that will intrigue the reader…"

~Turning Another Page

"Hot, sweet, dark thriller."

~Beth D

"It will keep you on the edge of your seat and give you chills."

~Escape Reality Book Blog

"Disturbing, haunting, sickly; yet hot, sexy and heart racing!"

~Amanda L

"From the first page [deMora] pulls you into the world she has created and you do not even try to escape…"

~Little Shop of Readers Blog

"A must read for all those dark, gritty romance fans out there."

~Sweet & Spicy Reads

"You will find yourself so drawn into the story that the outside world is blocked out and your locking the doors and turning on all the lights."

~Danena F

MariaLisa deMora

"Don't judge me for bonding with a vigilante
serial killer, she's more than what she does."
~iScream Books

"Thrilling...chilling...full of suspense, nail biting
edge of your seat excitement."
~Tracey H

"Every time MariaLisa deMora picks up her pen
(or opens her computer), she creates characters
you want to believe in."
~Gail S

"Intriguing dark storyline, beautiful love story
and nail-biting conclusion, what more could a
reader ask for?"
~Manda M

"This book takes you a dark and twisted ride
that is gripping..."
~Renee Entress' Blog

"This book is dark and gritty and I literally had
to take a day off from reading it because it's
that intense."
~My Girlfriend's Couch

"This is my favourite book so far from this
author ... I recommend this book if you enjoy
dark romantic thrillers."
~Cheekypee Reads and Reviews

"There's not enough stars to give this book and 5 just doesn't really do it justice!"

~DeLane C

"I couldn't put this book down from page one! Tried to stop & go to bed but couldn't sleep thinking about Alace and got up & finished the book."

~Debbie M

"MariaLisa DeMora, wordsmith that she is, made this a story of the enlightenment of a woman and finding love in a life where she has had none."

~Kat W

"Whatever deep dark trench [deMora] pulled a character like Alace from should be revisited again and often."

~Confessions of a Serial Reader

ADDITIONAL SERIES AND BOOKS

Please note that books in a series frequently feature characters from additional books within that series. If series books are read out of order, readers will twig to spoilers for the other books, so going back to read the skipped titles won't have the same angsty reveals.

Rebel Wayfarers MC series:

Mica, #1
A Sweet & Merry Christmas, #1.5
Slate, #2
Bear, #3
Jase, #4
Gunny, #5
Mason, #6
Hoss, #7
Harddrive Holidays, #7.5
Duck, #8
Biker Chick Campout, #8.5
Watcher, #9
A Kiss to Keep You, #9.25
Gun Totin' Annie, #9.5
Secret Santa, #9.75
Bones, #10
Gunny's Pups, #10.25
Never Settle, #10.5
Not Even A Mouse, #10.75
Fury, #11
Christmas Doings, #11.25
Gypsy's Lady, #11.5
Cassie, #12
Road Runner's Ride, #12.5

Occupy Yourself band series:

Born Into Trouble, #1
Grace In Motion, #2 (TBD)

What They Say, #3 (TBD)

Neither This, Nor That MC series:

This Is the Route Of Twisted Pain, #1
Treading the Traitor's Path: Out Bad, #2
Shelter My Heart, #3
Trapped by Fate on Reckless Roads, #4
Tarnished Lies and Dead Ends, #5

Rebel Wayfarers crossover stories:

Going Down Easy
No Man's Land
In Search of Solace
Puppy Love
Steel and Swagger

Mayhan Bucklers MC series:

Most Rikki-Tik, #1
Mad Minute, #2
Pucker Factor, #3
Boocoo Dinky Dau, #4

Borderline Freaks MC series:

Service and Sacrifice, #1
More Than Enough, #2
Lack of Inbetween, #3

See You in Valhalla, #4

Alace Sweets series:

Alace Sweets, #1
Seeking Worthy Pursuits, #2
Embarrassment of Monsters, #3
All the Broken Rules, #4

With My Whole Heart series:

With My Whole Heart, #1
Bet On Us, #2

If You Could Change One Thing:
Tangled Fates Stories

There Are Limits, #1
Rules Are Rules, #2
The Gray Zone, #3

Other Books:

Outlaw Heartstrings
Sidetracked Love
Only For You
Hard Focus
Salvaged Parts
Spark of the Lock
Dirty Bitches MC: Season 3

Steel and Swagger

More information available at
mldemora.com.

www.ingramcontent.com/pod-product-compliance
Lightning Source LLC
Chambersburg PA
CBHW060909210726
48293CB00006B/2027